WESTERN

P9-CRC-839

WITHDRAWN

DUE 14 DAY LOAN AYS

THE MARSHAL

Also by Lauran Paine
In Thorndike Large Print

TANNER

THE MARSHAL

Lauran Paine

Thorndike Press • Thorndike, Maine

Library of Congress Cataloging in Publication Data:

Paine, Lauran.
  The marshal.

  1. Large type books. I. Title
[PS3566.A34M3 1986b]   813'.54   85-24713
ISBN 0-89621-694-2 (lg. print : alk. paper)

All the characters and events portrayed in this story are fictitious.

Large Print edition available through arrangement with
Walker and Company, New York.

Cover design by Abby Trudeau.
Cover illustration by Deborah Pompano.

THE MARSHAL

He was a tall, lean, handsome man, tanned by sun and wind. He carried a blued Colt with ivory grips in a hand-carved black holster which matched the bullet belt it was attached to.

His hat had been formed with great care, the wide brim meticulously curved to the exact degree of upswept perfection most rangemen tried to achieve and rarely did.

His hatband, like his belt, was of carved leather and both bore sterling buckles, the one on his trouserbelt with golden initials: J D for Jack Padgett.

He was a stern individual of slow gravity and hard blue eyes. For three years he had been the marshal of Juniper — Piute Valley's only major town, named after the smelly little bristly trees that grew throughout the valley. He had been appointed by the Juniper town council after the previous marshal, old Jud Pruitt, had moved up to Wyoming to be near his married daughter.

Old Jud had been just about everything Jack Padgett was not. A square-built, bull-necked man who used his great strength and ham-sized fists more often than his gun, Jud used to play poker all night and drink whiskey with the stockmen on Saturday nights. Over the years he had brought in a few outlaws, but even his best friends around Piute Valley — and he'd had plenty of them — had never said Jud was an ideal lawman.

The second year of Padgett's tenure as Juniper town marshal, he broke up a fight at Arley Patton's saloon without removing his gloves or advancing any farther into the room than the doorway. He fired one shot into the ceiling, and the next shot directly at a drunken cowboy by the name of Cal Vincent, who swung to face Marshal Padgett with a snarl and a dipping right arm.

It was a justified killing, but it shocked the entire community. Old Jud would have rushed in, collared Cal Vincent from behind, lifted him by the scruff of the neck and the britches, and hurled him out into the roadway. Then he would have disarmed him and dragged him down to be locked up.

"Different fellers do things in different ways," Arley had said to the grim-faced cattlemen who had leaned on his bar, after Vincent had been buried over east of town on the little knob called Cemetery Hill.

Later, Arley also said Marshal Padgett would not be a good individual to cross. That judgment gradually spread well beyond town to the cow ranges.

There had not been a shooting or any serious trouble in town for a year after that killing. There had also been a slight distance established between the people of Juniper and their town marshal. No one ever joshed Marshal Padgett the way they had joshed Jud Pruitt. No one ever sat on the old bench out front of the jailhouse and spat tobacco juice into the dusty roadway while swapping tall tales the way they had done with Marshal Pruitt.

He kept order. He had faced down a few belligerent, usually drunken, cowboys, and he had pursued at least three fugitives passing through Piute Valley. Two of them he brought back belly-down, shot through the head. The third man had come back into town with arms tightly bound in back, legs lashed to his stirrup-leathers, face hanging down dripping blood from a savage beating.

9

Arley Patton clung stubbornly to his judgment of Marshal Padgett. He made only one concession as the years passed. "Nobody says you got to like him — but he sure does what he's drawin' wages to do. He keeps the law, by gawd."

Walt Nevins, owner of the general store, had a grandson who let his wagon loose in the roadway and the evening stage ran over it. Marshal Padgett walked over to where the little boy was crying as though his own heart would break. He took him and the broken wagon down to Donald Myser's blacksmith shop, borrowed tools and, with the help of the little boy, worked until after dark repairing the wagon.

Afterwards, at the saloon, Don told them that Marshal Padgett had laughed with the kid and showed him how to match wood and all. Don settled his mighty frame against the bar shaking his head in near-disbelief. "He treated that kid like they was old friends. Never lost patience, not once."

One of the stockmen fixed Don Myser with a flinty squint. "Yeah, but did he fix the wagon?"

Don raised his dark eyes to the cowman. "Like new. So help me Hannah, he used them tools and done that work better'n I could've done."

Nothing more was said for a long time. Men drank, shifted their feet, and leaned on the bar

10

trying to reconcile this fresh thing they had learned about their iron lawman with what else they knew of him — like the killing of Cal Vincent.

Arley Patton reiterated his earlier pronouncement. "Different folks do things different."

Burt Standish, rangeboss for the Patterson ranch, scowled at Arley. Cal Vincent had worked for Burt. "Fixin' a kid's wagon don't change him shootin' Cal when he was so damned drunk he didn't know which way he was facing."

That remark jangled some nerves. The silence deepened until Walt Nevins walked in. Several sets of eyes followed Walt from the door to the bar, where he waited for Arley to set up his Old Bushmills and a jolt glass.

Walt was a pale man who wore rimless glasses and had very little hair. He did not remove his black cotton sleeve-protectors even after he'd locked the store and gone home for supper. He was wearing them now as he filled the glass, dropped the whiskey straight down, and blew out a ragged breath.

He turned watery pale blue eyes toward the other drinkers and started to tell the story of his grandson and Marshal Padgett.

Buck Standish interrupted him. "We know all about it," he growled.

Walt Nevins was not to be stopped, but he

11

turned off in a new direction. "Jamie came home this evening like he'd just met the White Knight."

A half-breed rangerider looked baffled. "Met *who*?" he called from the upper end of the bar. Two companions turned toward him from opposite sides and started explaining.

Walt Nevins said, "Every boy needs a hero, gents."

No one said a word. Walt's grandson and his mother had returned to Juniper from somewhere up north in Colorado or Wyoming, having been abandoned by their father and husband, an itinerant rider by the name of Dick Arnett. Jamie hadn't had a hero in his father for a damned fact.

Flinty old Jeremiah Macklin, who owned a large outfit due west from town, looked down into his empty glass with a dark frown. "Walt, the lad'd do better to pick on someone else for his hero."

Nevins turned stiffly. "Who, Mister Macklin?"

Neither old Jeremiah nor anyone else replied. Obviously Walt Nevins was now also a defender of Marshal Padgett.

So was Don Myser the blacksmith. So was Arley Patton, but that was about the length of the list. None of the cattlemen had forgotten

12

what they knew had been an unnecessary killing, and the others, who had never taken a real stand one way or another, did not take one now. There had been those two dead outlaws shot between the eyes, and that third one beaten half to death and brought down Main Street behind the erect lawman on his handsome chestnut horse, semi-conscious and still dripping blood half a day after he had been whipped.

It began to rain the day after Marshal Padgett fixed the wagon, and it did not stop for five days. The roads were not usable, buildings were clammy, and very little business was transacted. Merchants dragged out their duckboards for housewives who needed to shop and who otherwise could not cross Main Street, because it consisted of six inches of chocolaty mud that gummed up their feet and got very heavy by the time they reached the far plankwalk.

Arley did a little business among the townsmen, but none at all among the rangemen. He kept his cannon-heater crackling. There were several day-long card games, and one poker session that lasted the full five days of the downpour with fresh players relieving the jaded ones.

Marshal Padgett did not cross on the duckboards but he showed himself, usually attired in a black-and-red-checkered blanket coat over his blue work shirt, britches stuffed into the tops of his shiny boots to keep them from gathering mud, and as always, wearing his skintight black doeskin roping gloves and the handsome ivory-stocked six-gun in its carved black holster.

He went down to Jim Danforth's livery and trading barn, which was on the same side of the road as his jailhouse-office, and he went in the opposite direction up to Sam Starr's saddle and harness works, also on his side of the road.

When he finally crossed over to Nevin's store because he was out of his special brand of cheroots, it was the seventh day and the rain had stopped. The road was almost dry and sunshine burned downward, making it possible to cross the roadway if people knew where the hard places were and walked very carefully.

Juniper was recovering a full week from that deluge. In its wake, with the roads hard again, stockmen arrived with their wagons for the supplies they had been short of when the storm hit, travel was resumed, and people got busy again. Walt Nevins hired the town's carpenter and undertaker, Swen Jorgenson, to climb to the roof of his store and find the leak which had dripped water onto his wood stove, making a sound like frying meat each time a big drop of water landed on the hot iron top of the stove.

14

Marshal Padgett paid for a full box of his special stogies and leaned on the counter with Walt, discussing the recent storm, weather in general, and how such things as downpours affected business. Marshal Padgett seemed to be concerned for the town's economy, not just in keeping order. Walt Nevins approved of that, too, in the tall, handsome lawman.

Padgett went up to Arley's place and paid for a jolt of malt whiskey. It had been Arley's observation that Marshal Padgett did not like whisky. Arley had been a saloonman for almost thirty years; he knew people quite well. Padgett always ordered one jolt, paid for it in advance, then steeled himself to down it. Afterward, his expression was of stone. He would not even allow his eyes to blink. But he never ordered a second jolt and he never accepted drinks from men who offered him one.

When the whisky bottle had been removed, Arley smiled and said, "Things'll pick up now, with the ground hard again and all them stockmen been holed up on their ranches for a week or more."

Marshal Padgett lighted one of his cheroots, held it between his teeth, and tugged at his gloves before replying. "I reckon," he replied softly, and raised his eyes. "As long as they mind their manners."

15

Arley bobbed his head about that and watched the tall, lean, handsome man stroll back out into the sunshine. Arley was divorced and lived up at the roominghouse on the ground floor only about three rooms north of Marshal Padgett's room. Even before he had started defending the town marshal, he had been impressed by how clean and freshly shaved the town marshal always was. Arley thought it probably cost Marshal Padgett a fair slice of his wages to be like that. No one else in town went to all that trouble to project an image of cleanliness, resolution and duty.

A man like that had to be respected. Getting laundry done in Juniper had never been easy. It still wasn't. There were only three women in town who would take in wash and also do ironing. For most unmarried men, the cost was bothersome and so was bundling things up and trotting out among the houses behind town to deliver them. When this was normally done by the unmarried men in Juniper, the usual reason was because they had reached a point where they could no longer stand themselves; they had worn everything they owned at least six times.

2

That five-day downpour seemed to mark the end of spring and the beginning of summer because for the ensuing three weeks the sky was clear, the sun shone, grass fairly leapt from the earth while around the town birds noisily went about stealing string, horsehair, fighting one another for territory, and making nests. They also did other things, such as fluttering their wings a lot, which fascinated little boys and horrified their mothers who herded them indoors to do homework, or something anyway.

Outfits like the Macklin and Patterson ranches, which were west and northwest of Juniper, had fleshed out their riding crews early and were up to their hocks in work. The attendant and customary injuries Doc Winthrop cared for either at his cottage in town or by commuting out to the ranches in his old top-buggy with the rusty red running gear.

There were a number of things which arrived along with the crocuses. Flinty old Jeremiah Macklin sent two of his riders out to fetch in fresh horses to replace the animals his four riders had been using hard for the past two weeks, and the riders came back as solemn as owls. The Macklin remuda of loose stock was gone.

Old Jeremiah belonged to that earlier generation that took care of its own problems. But he sent a man to town for Marshal Padgett before taking his remaining three riders, all armed to the gills, in hot pursuit. Jeremiah was shrewd; he knew exactly what he would do if he found the horsethieves; however, since it was no longer possible to just lynch outlaws where one found them without getting into serious trouble with the law, a man had to seem at least to be conforming to the new, and contemptible, way things were.

It was nine miles from the Macklin ranch to Juniper and nine miles back for his rider and the marshal. With that much of a lead and only a little luck Macklin would have found his horses and the thieves before Marshal Padgett even got close. It had never been difficult to provoke outlaws into a battle, especially with cattlemen carrying ropes. Fighting clear was the only chance they had and over the years outlaws had come to bitterly know that.

They found the trail without difficulty. It was impossible to hide fifteen horse tracks; the answer was to raid a ranch at night and depend upon speed to do the rest.

The tracks led northward toward the bald foothills directly across Patterson ranch's west range, close enough to the buildings and the ranchyard for the drive to have been heard.

But evidently it wasn't heard.

Old Macklin was on a good trail and did not go over to the yard. Instead he sent one of his riders. It would be up to this man and Burt Standish to catch up.

Macklin half-hoped they would not be able to. Not in time anyway. He was a crabbed old man of sinew and bone, not quite average height without a spare ounce of grease on him anywhere. He said he was sixty but the old-timers around Piute Valley scoffed; he had to be at least seventy they said. Macklin was a widower, and he had never had children, which was probably just as well. He never smiled, never let up on his lifelong obsession with building up the quality of his cattle and the size of his landed holdings. Over the years it was rumored he had accomplished the latter with fire and bullets.

He was as unforgiving as the devil, as relentless as God and, so they said anyway, had ice water for blood. He was also something else: For more than half a century he had fought the weather, Indians, outlaws, sometimes his neighbors, and he never forgot the lessons these encounters had taught him. So right now as he jogged stiffly over the trail of the men who had run off his loose stock, he told the leathery-faced cowboy at his side what the tracks had told him.

"Four of 'em. Horseshoes danged near wore through. They come a long way and they know where they're going, an' if they're as far off as I expect they didn't see us cross the open country into these little hills."

The cowboy was narrowly watching the onward country. If there were indeed four outlaws up there somewhere, then he and the only remaining rider, plus old Jeremiah, were outnumbered. And, if the old cuss was wrong about not being seen, the three of them might right-this-minute be riding down someone's gun barrel into an ambush. The cowboy leaned on his saddlehorn to address his employer without taking his narrowed eyes off the onward, uneven flow of countryside. The foothills trailed off toward a distant rise of forested uplands and he didn't like the looks of that.

"Maybe we better slack off a little, Mister

Macklin. Let Standish catch up. If them fellers is sittin' up yonder in the timber they'll see us sure as hell. And there's only us two fellers and you."

Jeremiah turned his grainy old face with its lipless slash of a mouth, its beaked nose and its flinty eyes. "They ain't in the trees. They've been bearing northeast for the last few miles. . . . An' I can smell an ambush."

That ended the discussion for a solid hour, until they followed the curving tracks around the shoulder of the timbered slope exactly as old Macklin had predicted and were heading toward a big sunken bowl with tall grass and hardwood trees growing luxuriantly in all directions. The sunken place was perhaps three or four hundred acres in size. His riders had never been up here before but Jeremiah had.

"It's called the Sink," he informed them, squinting dead ahead. "It's the only water and decent feed for fifty miles, and sure as hell them boys knew it was up there."

His companions said nothing. They shared a disquieting thought that perhaps the horse-thieves were still up there. They had been riding hard since leaving the ranchyard, and the sun was high, making a faint bluish haze in the distance. Jeremiah slackened to a slogging walk, tucked a cud of tobacco into his leathery cheek, spat amber, and slouched along on a loose rein as he said, "Damned fools. Anyone'd know better than to stop even to blow the livestock this close to where they stole 'em."

Both his companons straightened a little. So far old Jeremiah had been right; if he was correct now too, the outlaws were up in that low place — and they had been crossing open country for an hour. Even careless outlaws would have noted their arrival in the area by now. One rider glanced worriedly over his shoulder. There was dust but it was a long way back. He drew Jeremiah's attention to this and the old man twisted briefly, then straightened forward again. "That'll be Standish." He was about to say more when the second cowboy raised a rigid arm. "Hell, look yonder. Someone is riding south from the upper edge of that sunken place. Gawddamn; if there's four up yonder restin' then this here feller makes it five, Mister Macklin, and them are real bad odds." The cowboy lowered his arm. "We better wait a bit."

The two rangeriders halted without waiting to see what old Jeremiah would do. He turned a fierce look upon them, but said nothing. Finally he reined to a halt also because he had no choice; if his riders would not keep going he could not do much by himself except maybe get killed.

He spat in outrage. In his younger days men who were in the right, and sometimes when they were not, never hesitated no matter what the gawddamned odds. Punky, that's what folks had got to be — gutless and punky. He let the reins hang slack while he and his two riders sat watching that very distant, solitary horseman riding in plain sight and at a dead walk down deeper into the sunken place.

At that distance there was little they could make out except that he was riding slowly. Jeremiah cursed. "He'll see us settin' out here like squirrels on a rock." Jeremiah twisted again. The dust was closer which meant that the Patterson Ranch rangeboss and his crew, along with Jeremiah's messenger, were rapidly closing the gap. He settled forward and said, "We got 'em. It'll be a horse race but we got 'em. They been ridin' hard all night. They don't have the horseflesh under 'em to keep it up."

The day was brilliant, distances were faintly blurred, a solitary red-tailed hawk was making widening sweeps high overhead, a rigid fat hedgehog was watching the three riders without blinking, and without any warning there was a flat, high-pitched gunshot. A Winchester gunshot. It's echo was swallowed in the vastness. One of Macklin's riders sprang from the saddle and yanked out his own saddlegun, but

23

the bullet had not been aimed in their direction, evidently, because that solitary distant rider veered off and also fired. They could see the dirty puff of black-powder smoke.

He set his big horse into an easy lope and with a Winchester to his right shoulder seemed to be guiding the horse with his knees as he came ahead but never from the same side. He rode left then right, then left again, steadily sweeping closer to a nest of old dying trees whose roots were rotting underground where an invisible river ran.

Smoke puffs arose from among the dying old trees. Jeremiah and his companions were transfixed, unable to comprehend what they were watching. It made no sense; they had already decided that the fifth rider was one of the outlaws – yet he was firing steadily into their resting place as he loped toward them. His big chestnut horse never disobeyed the rider's knees. It was as though he were blind and deaf, had no idea there were bullets seeking him and his rider. It was the damnedest performance old Macklin or his riders had ever seen.

The oncoming rider slammed the carbine into its boot and used his six-gun as he rode straight at the forted-up horsethieves. It took an exceptionally brave individual to stand in the face of something like this, and one horsethief finally sprang up and ran. The horseman dropped him with one bullet through the back.

Jeremiah forgot his cud, his companions, and even Buck Standish with the Patterson-ranch riding crew when they swept up on winded horses, slammed to a halt, and stood in their stirrups to watch.

The last gunshot, twice as loud and deep as the Winchesters had been, was fired as the horseman rode in among the trees and aimed at something standing directly in front of his horse.

Then he halted and in plain sight of the on-lookers looped the reins and began reloading the six-gun from his belt. Buck Standish eased down in the saddle. "Jesus...Jeremiah, do you know who that is?"

Macklin spat and continued to watch the distant figure without saying a word.

"That's the marshal from town," Standish said softly. "Sure as I'm settin' here that's him....Let's go up there."

Jeremiah spat, then said, "Set right where you are." Slowly he turned his head toward Buck Standish. Buck said, "That last one, did you see him? He come up off the ground with his hands over his head."

If the others had seen that man get killed they were certainly not going to say so. Standish

25

repeated what he had said before. "Let's go on up there."

Macklin's eyes glowed behind slitted flesh. "I told you, set right where you are. Let him come down to us. You don't ride up onto a man under these circumstances, Buck. You leave that up to him. . . . Yes, I seen that last one get shot, and if you'd like a little advice — don't none of you ever mention a word about that. Not a damned word. Not even in your sleep."

They sat. In the middle distance the horseman had dismounted to water his horse. He then went among the dead men bending over from time to time, but at that distance no one could be sure of what he was doing. Old Jeremiah, though, made a bleak, cruel smile. He seemed to know. One of the riders said, "Collectin' their guns," and Jeremiah spat in scorn. "Riflin' their pockets for identification. You can't collect no bounty money with just guns."

Finally, the horseman mounted, reined around in their direction, and rode leisurely toward them. He studied them as he approached, and they studied him. When he was closer they saw him fish forth a cheroot from his coat, light it, and trickle a little smoke.

He wasn't even sweating, although his face was faintly flushed when he halted in front of them and returned their gazes. He removed the cigar to address old Jeremiah. "Are those your horses, Mister Macklin?"

Jeremiah jerked his head up and down without parting his lips.

"They're scattered a little," Marshal Padgett said calmly, looking down his nose at the older man, "but you can round them up. . . . And you can fetch the horsethieves to town in a wagon to be buried, if you'd do that."

Jeremiah's head jerked up and down again. Then he spat and said, "How in the hell did you know they was my horses and that them fellers had stole them?"

"Yesterday. . . I got word," the tall handsome man said, and raised his black-gloved left hand with the reins in it to ride on. One of Standish's men grinned and said, "Marshal, if you're ever of a mind to sell that big horse I'd sure put my soul in hock to buy him."

Jack Padgett gazed at the man's sweaty, smiling face, lifted his lips a fraction and rode on without speaking.

They twisted to watch. Padgett's big chestnut horse was slogging along on a loose rein at a steady walk, head-down-relaxed.

Jeremiah finally jettisoned the cud and got stiffly down from his saddle. The other men also dismounted. Buck Standish, who had lost a rider to that blued six-shooter with the ivory

27

handles and for that, among other reasons, did not like Marshal Padgett, tipped his hat forward, wearing an expression which defied description.

Old Jeremiah was the first to shake off the mood. He faced toward the dying trees and said, "Well Buck, I expect you can lend a hand lugging them dead men down to my place and we'll take 'em into town in a wagon, like he said." Jeremiah looked at one of his riders. "Afterward you'n Buster round up the horses and drive them home."

A younger man who had peach fuzz on his cheeks instead of whiskers looked at Buck, the man he rode for. "I didn't see no one stand up. . . . Did he really do that, Buck?"

Jeremiah fixed the youth with a malevolent glare. "Sonny, you listen real good to me. You never saw nothing. All you know is that he come onto them from the north and they fired first, and after that he shot it out with them fair and square. . . . Boy, you start talkin' about other things that maybe happened out there," Jeremiah paused to rake them all with a bitter stare. "A man like that don't wait. You try'n put a bad name to him, and he'll kill you on sight, and you better remember that. . . . Now let's go get the horses and those dead fellers."

3

The days had been getting slightly longer for a month now. Sometimes the heat lingered too, making it very pleasant for folks to go for a walk after dusk. It also made it difficult for mothers to round up their offspring when bedtime arrived whether it was still light out or not.

Marshal Padgett was sitting at his dusted and orderly desk with the jailhouse door open in case a little breeze came through town, smoking and eyeing Doctor Winthrop, who was his antithesis. Doc did not smoke, he chewed. He never seemed to have his shirts ironed nor his pants pressed. His hair was all unruly grey thatch and his little blue eyes beneath an overhanging brow were direct, shrewd and disillusioned. He had performed four autopsies for which he would not be paid because the town council had not authorized them, nor had any

29

next of kin if there were any. Doc had performed them out of simply curiosity.

He sat gazing at the handsome town marshal, admiring the shiny badge which Padgett had inherited from Jud Pruitt. Doc had known Pruitt twenty-five years and not once in that length of time had he seen that badge shined.

He said, "Well, Swen'll get paid for the coffins and I'll get expenses for the embalming acid. They had been riding good horses, Marshal, but the rest of it wasn't worth much."

Marshal Padgett trickled smoke. "Damned fools, Doctor. If they hadn't got it up there they'd have got it somewhere else before long."

Doc agreed with part of that statement because he had always believed outlaws were damned fools. *Any* outlaws. He shifted slightly on the chair, eyes drifting to the dully shining guns in the wall rack. The story he had disbelieved at first, had been repeated to his face by Mister Macklin, so now Doc believed it. He said, "In my lifetime I've buried three lawmen. Two in Missouri, one up in Wyoming. All three of them died for taking unnecessary chances. A man's only got one life, Marshal."

Jack Padgett removed the cheroot and tapped off the grey ash. "Chances go with the job, Doctor, and what might seem to you to be unnecessary risks, mostly aren't risks at all."

Doc's eyes widened on the lawman. "According to what I heard, you rode right at them . . . four of them among some trees."

Padgett plugged the cigar back between his even white teeth, his eyes returning to Winthrop's face. "They were already in trouble. Macklin was behind them out of rifle range but in plain sight. Farther back there was dust where more men were coming. They didn't even notice me until I was almost in carbine range then one of them got excited and fired. The distance was too great, until I ran at them."

Doc's eyes did not even blink. "Face on?"

Padgett nodded.

"One of 'em was shot right through the middle of the back, Marshal."

Padgett's gaze darkened noticeably. "Doctor, if you've never been under fire like that you wouldn't understand how a man can be aiming at someone facing him and pull the trigger as the man suddenly whips around to run."

Doc Winthrop seemed to accept that. At any rate he left the office shortly afterward bound for Arley's saloon. He belonged to a loose brotherhood of Thursday-night poker players. He passed two people on his way over there who spoke and Doc did not even hear them.

Marshal Padgett put on his hat and made a round of town. He ended up over behind the

31

public corrals near the northern boundary of Juniper and leaned in the warm, beautiful evening to wait.

The Nevins house was east of him on down the road a few hundred yards. It had two stories like several other houses in town, and lights showed both upstairs and downstairs. When the upstairs light winked out Marshal Padgett turned slowly and leaned so that he could see down in that direction.

The silhouette was faint at first, then assumed a rounded, firm substance. When Walt Nevins's wife had been alive it had been her idea to name her new baby Antoinette, but she had never been called anything but Bessie.

Bessie was a sweet woman with trustful china blue eyes. She was almost twenty years younger than the handsome town marshal. If her bitter experience with the rangerider she had married and borne a son by had affected her, it did not show. People liked her and not because they felt sorry for her. She was a pretty little thing with hair like corn silk and a complexion like her mother's had been — peaches and cream.

She smiled until her eyes were nearly closed and held out a hand to Marshal Padgett. He held her fingers lightly, drew her closer in the shadows and asked how Jamie was.

She leaned closer until they were touching

before replying that her son was fine, and that he had drawn a picture of Marshal Padgett to hang on his bedroom wall. Now, she said, he wanted her to buy him a cap gun with white handles.

Softly smiling, the marshal lighted a cheroot and leaned against the corral stringers. "Beautiful night," he said, and when she agreed he also said he'd rented a buggy for tomorrow night if she'd care to go buggy-riding with him.

She liked the idea. She said she would bring some cold chicken if he'd like that. He drew on the cigar before answering that he was partial to fried chicken, then he asked if her father would mind looking after Jamie and her eyes seemed to be considering him in a different way for a moment before she said she did not think her father would mind at all.

He had to make a round of the town, he told her, and with a light touch of his fingers across her cheek, he smiled then walked back around the corner leaving her looking after him, some of the girlishness gone out of her face.

At Arley's saloon the customers were mostly from around town. Not for another two nights would the rangemen ride in for their Saturday-night visit.

When Marshal Padgett came through the spindle doors some of the conversation was dampened. Arley set up the marshal's private bottle of sipping whisky along with a sparkling clean glass and boomed a heartfelt greeting. Don Myser was leaning nearby and nodded his head as Padgett stepped up and filled the little glass. He downed the whisky neat and did not so much as blink. Myser leaned slightly and lowered his voice. "Good thing I overheard them boys talkin' outside the shop, eh, Marshal?"

Padgett gazed at the shorter, thicker man. "Good thing. Macklin was happy to get his horses back."

Don nodded. "And that's four more won't make life miserable for decent folks no more."

Padgett gazed around the room. It was faintly foggy from tobacco smoke. There was a poker game in progress over behind the cannon-heater, and Doc's shock of silver hair showed among the players. Otherwise trade was light tonight. He tugged at his gloves, nodded to the blacksmith, and walked back outside.

Doc raised his head to watch him depart, and had to be reminded it was his turn to deal cards before he turned back.

Down at Danforth's barn a man was balancing on a rickety chair lighting the carriage lamps, which were bolted on either side of the doorless front opening. Up the road a ways at Sam Starr's harness works, two lamps with clean mantles were also burning and Sam was visible through the front window at his big work table. At the stage company's corralyard north of the harness works, a coach was parked out front with no horses on the pole. Two hostlers were loading small crates inside where passengers normally sat. The stage company did some light freighting along with hauling passengers. The voices of the loaders carried clearly in the warm, still night. They were discussing the killing of those four outlaws, and they were both enormously impressed with the way Marshal Padgett had taken on all four.

Padgett strolled over to the jailhouse to finish writing the letters he had started earlier, before Doctor Winthrop had walked in.

The total in rewards was three thousand dollars. If Arley Patton had known that he probably would have reflected that a man could get an awful lot of shirts washed and ironed for three thousand dollars.

Jim Danforth, who owned the livery and trading barn, walked in because he had seen the marshal's lamp burning. Jim was a bull-necked, barrel-chested older man with a drooping paunch which hid the top button of his britches. He too smoked cigars, but the ones Jim Danforth smoked smelled like burning hair at branding time.

Padgett had almost completed his letters when Jim entered the little office. He looked up without smiling; he wanted to get those letters on the night stage.

Danforth took a chair uninvited and said, "Thought you might be interested to know, Marshal, that the brand on one of them horses those outlaws was riding was a flying W."

Padgett said nothing.

"The feller who dungs out for me comes from Wyoming. He recognized that mark right off. It's some big outfit near a place called Tie Siding, not too far north of the Colorado line. He said they keep an awful lot of horses, hire about ten riders during the season, and run several thousand cows."

Marshal Padgett listened impassively and picked up his pen, holding it poised during the silence between them. Jim Danforth got red in the face and pushed up out of the chair, nodded, and stalked out into the night.

Padgett finished the letter. He identified the four outlaws by name according to the things he had taken from their pockets. Frank Ballester, Fritz Hahn, Charley Simpson and Dick Arnett.

He sealed the letters, crossed over to the slot in front of the general store, dropped them in, and headed for the rooming house to bed down.

Just before dropping off to sleep, he heard the northbound stage passing at a dead walk with chain-tugs jangling. They always emptied the mailbox last before hitching up for the night run northward. And for the last three years they had been obeying the town ordinance which prohibited coach drivers from entering or leaving Juniper at any gait faster than a walk.

The following morning, three dusty range-riders came into town from the south, put up their horses at Danforth's place, beat off dust, studied the town, then headed for the cafe. They were more or less alike — rangy, lean men who needed shaves and a shearing. They had old boots, old hats, scarred saddles, weathered young-old faces and a loose-jointed way of moving.

A little earlier, about the time of that five-day rain the previous month, itinerant riders looking for work had been common at both the cafe and the saloon. Since then, though, with most bunkhouses full, there had not been very many saddle tramps around town.

Marshal Padgett was over at Sam Starr's shop and did not see the strangers arrive. Sam had been working on a hand-carved saddle for Padgett and during the moments when he was alone in the shop, Sam, who had never married, blamed himself aloud for ever agreeing to do the job. If he'd had any inkling that Marshal Padgett was so damned persnickity he wouldn't have taken it on.

But with the marshal leaning over the counter Sam was obliging. More than obliging. By Sam Starr's count Jack Padgett had killed seven men since he'd come to town three years ago.

Padgett did not want a conventional double rig. His rigging had to be seven-eighths because, he explained to Sam, full double rigging cut a horse just behind his upper forelegs. Sam nodded his head without meeting Padgett's gaze. Sam had been manufacturing full double-rigged saddles for thirty years. As far as he knew no damned horse had ever lost his front legs by being chewed through by a cinch ring snugged up to a double rig.

Three weeks later Sam Starr came to the solemn realization that Marshal Padgett had been right: A seven-eighths rig was better than a full double rig, but by then it didn't matter.

Padgett went over to the cafe after visiting with Sam. The counter was empty. The cafeman said three strangers had walked out no more than ten minutes earlier, the last of his breakfast customers.

Padgett ate heartily then went down to Danforth's place, saddled his big handsome chestnut horse, and rode southeastward out of town. Jim Danforth stood sullenly in the alley watching him depart. All he'd been trying to do last night was help the marshal know a little more about those four horsethieves he'd shot. He sure wasn't like Jud Pruitt. Old Jud would have been pleased to listen.

Doctor Winthrop came down for his rig with the rusty running gear and because Jim was still irritated he told Doc of his cold reception last night at the jailhouse office.

Doc was noncommittal. "He was probably busy, Jim."

"Yeah," grumbled the horsetrader. "Writing two letters to someone up in Cheyenne. Letters is somethin' it don't make much difference whether you finish 'em today or tomorrow." Jim sighed and straightened his face. "Another baby, Doc?"

"No. On a day as pretty as this one I thought I'd just plain go for a drive without having to hurry some place."

They went together to pull Doc's rig out of the wagon shed, and while Jim was waiting for his dayman to fetch Doc's horse, he settled into a forgiving frame of mind. "Yeah, I guess he was busy. I know for a fact writin' letters is harder work for me than harnessing a hitch of mules."

Doc helped with the California harness and had to endure another series of profane criticisms by Jim Danforth about a horse harness that relied on a breast strip instead of orthodox collar pads and collar.

They were out in the back alley with Doc hoisting himself up while Jim stood at the mare's bit. "Which way?" Jim said.

Doc was sifting the lines through his fingers to get them even when he answered. "Northwest. Out toward the Macklin place."

Jim stepped aside. "Have a nice ride," he said, and half waved a thick hand as Doc drove away.

The sun was still climbing. Unless Doc piddled the time away he could be back to town in time for supper. Jim returned to his barn runway and leaned on a half-door watching his dayman dunging out. "Did you hear the names of them outlaws the marshal shot, Sam?"

The hostler answered without raising his head or missing a motion with his manure fork. "No. And there wasn't names on the headboards Swen stuck up on Cemetery Hill. Just the date they got killed and the word 'Horsethief.' I guess Marshal Padgett'd be the only one who might know. Even Doc wouldn't if the marshal cleaned out their pockets before they was brought into town. . . . Why? Does it matter?

40

You maybe related to one of them, Jim?"

Danforth eyed his hired man woodenly. That was what you got nowadays. If they weren't drunks or thieves they were smart alecks. He pushed off the door heading for his harness room where he had a tiny desk, a chair, and some ledgers he hated with an abiding passion, and which he did not maintain well. Nonetheless he did keep them, otherwise he would never know whether he was making money or not. Not exactly; Jim had been a trader all his mature years. He knew when he was running in the black, but such was the nature of a horsetrader that he could not bring himself to lie even to his own books.

4

Jeremiah Macklin would have been out with his riders when Doctor Winthrop arrived in his yard except for a troublesome leg which had been pestering him with increasing frequency the past few days. When Doc arrived Jeremiah was leaning on the tie-rack in front of the barn, waiting. He had seen Doc's rig, had recognized it by the red running gear, and normally old Jeremiah would have been suspicious about the medical man driving out this far. Today he was at first surprised, then relieved, and by the time Doc halted his mare at the rack and climbed down, Jeremiah was grateful. Doc's arrival had saved him a drive to town.

He helped take the mare from between the shafts and stall her while he and Doc discussed the weather, range conditions, prospects for summer rain, and a snippet or two of gossip

Doc had brought with him from town. Then they headed for the broad, long veranda of the main house and Doc finally said, "Why are you favoring your leg, Jeremiah?" And that was what old Macklin had been waiting to hear. He launched into a description of his symptoms, shook the leg a little going up the steps, and eased it out in front with exaggerated caution before easing his carcass down into a chair.

Doc fished for his plug and gnawed off a corner. He said, "How old are you?" and Jeremiah's flinty eyes sparked. "What'n hell's that got to do with my leg, Doc?"

"It may have everything to do with it," reported Doc, with his own show of irritation.

"I'm healthy as a bull, Doc."

"Yeah. Bulls wear out and so do men. Jeremiah, I'd guess you got what everyone gets sooner or later if they spend most of their lives outside, summer and winter, rain and heat, snow and what-not. The Lumbago."

Old Macklin's flinty face hardened in bleak thought. Finally he said, "Seventy-three. And that's no one's damned business but yours and mine."

Doc stroked his chin to control the smile. "It'll help if you're honest with me. I can't do much for folks who aren't. . . . Stay out of the cold, Jeremiah. I don't mean this year but next

43

winter and the winters after that. And—"

"How in the tarnation hell does a man stay out of the cold and run a cattle outfit at the same time?"

Doc fixed the older man with his professional stare. "That's for you to figure out. *My* leg is all right. I'm just tellin' you what you've got to do. Whether you do it or not is up to you. I'll leave you some medicine when I head back. But it's not goin' to do much if you don't help it work."

Macklin looked relieved. "You got it with you?"

"In the satchel in my rig. How close was Marshal Padgett to that feller shot through the head when he fired at him?"

Jeremiah blinked twice, swung his gaze away, then back. He had been caught totally unprepared for that question. He finally gave a gruff reply. "We was a long way south, Doc. Too far to make out the details. Why?"

"And the one he shot in the back..."

Now old Jeremiah was collected, and he looked steadily at Doctor Winthrop, his grainy old face hardening. They had known each other a long time, since Doc had arrived in the country from up in Wyoming. They had shared a few bottles since those earlier days and a number of all-night poker sessions. Macklin had

44

never in his long life gone out of his way to make friends for the sake of having them, but he liked Doctor Winthrop; moreover, he respected him.

He loosened a little and said, "How about some malt whisky?"

Doc shook his head. "No thanks, but if you want to, go right ahead."

Macklin did not move from his chair and when he looked at Doc, Winthrop's shrewd eyes were still fixed upon him. He sighed. "What are you doin', Doc? Let sleepin' dogs lie. . . . You know that kind of a man as well as I do."

Doc slouched in his chair and ran a slow look down across the golden-lighted, silent and empty, big ranch yard. "Jeremiah," he said quietly. "First there was Vincent, that man who rode for Burt Standish. Then there was a couple of outlaws shot square through the forehead at close range — they had powder burns. Then there was these four, one back-shot, the other one most likely with his hands in the air when Padgett shot him through the head."

Jeremiah gave a little start. "Hands in the air? What the hell are you talkin' about? Who told you such a story, anyway?"

Doc brought his gaze back to Macklin's face

45

and started to sputter again. Then Doc said, "Nobody told me, Jeremiah. When Marshal Padgett brought in those two dead ones he shot in the face, and their companion, who had been damned near beaten to death with a gun-barrel—"

"Doc, you better get off this subject," exclaimed old Macklin, leaning tensely forward in his chair. Doctor Winthrop continued as though Macklin had not spoken.

"It took me two days to get that beaten man so's he could talk and eat solid food. He went to prison with wounds that'll scar him for life. . . . He told me the other two had their hands in the air and Marshal Padgett didn't even get off his horse — he shot them both at close range through the head. Jeremiah, all I want from you is to verify what I think happened to that fourth horsethief, and don't tell me you were too far off. You told me the other night in town how he rode right down at them, and how he shot it out with them. You saw it all or you wouldn't have been able to tell me those details. . . . That one he shot through the forehead — were his hands in the air when Marshal Padgett killed him?"

Old Macklin started to spring from the chair in agitation, but the pain from the troublesome leg shot upward from his hip the full length of his spine making him gasp, then lock his jaw as he eased back again. When most of the pain subsided he glared and said, "What are you trying to do, you darned old fool? Piute Valley's needed a workin' lawman for fifteen years and now that we got one..." Macklin paused, pulled down a big breath and resumed, leaning now and speaking in a quiet, fierce tone of voice. "Doc, a horsethief is a horsethief. I'm not goin' to tell you anything and neither is anyone else." Macklin's flinty expression gradually softened a little and his tone of voice did the same. He eased back in the chair. "We been friends a long time.... What happened is done with. They're buried, I got my animals back.... I'll tell you one thing; I sure was surprised when I recognized him up there. I got no idea how he knew they were up there and I'm not going to ask. He did exactly right."

Doc remained slouched in his chair. "All right, he did exactly right, he shot it out with four outlaws and killed every one of them."

Jeremiah's eyes widened a trifle. "You never saw anything like it. He rode sashayin' and shootin' an' he never once stopped nor even ducked down. He rode right into them. My gawd I never saw the like an' I've seen my share of..." Jeremiah wagged his head.

Doc spat out his chewing cud and got settled

back in the chair again. "Listen to me, Jeremiah. Cal Vincent..."

Macklin's eyes returned to their normal squint. He considered his scarred, work-swollen hands.

"You didn't like it and neither did anyone else," Doc stated. "Vincent was so drunk—"

"Aw hell, he'd had a few but he wasn't—"

"Don't you tell me what he was or wasn't, Jeremiah. I autopsied him. He had so much alcohol in his blood he couldn't have found his butt with both hands."

"He was going for his gun, Doc, and that's a fact."

Winthrop stared at old Macklin. "You were one of the first rangemen to raise hell about that killing. You and Burt, and you were the loudest."

Old Macklin shifted his painful leg with great care and did not raise his eyes. "I'll tell you what you're doing," he told Winthrop in a soft tone. "You're fixin' to get yourself killed, Doc." His narrowed eyes came up slowly. "Listen to me; that son of a bitch is dead. He was a horsethief and in my book, there's nothin' lower nor meaner nor more worthless than a horsethief. You can't bring him back. I doubt if you even know his name or where he's from. Now you go askin' around and it's goin' to get back to Marshal Padgett eventually. He's not the kind of a man to do somethin' like that with. Take my word for it, Doc, I've known a few like him."

"Killers, Jeremiah?"

Just for a second old Macklin met Doc's gaze without moving, then he bobbed his head. Then, despite the pain it cost him, he shoved up to his feet and said, "Come inside and we'll rassle somethin' to eat and mix a little whisky and water. . . . Doc, I don't want to hear no more talk like this. Not ever. An' if you start again I'm goin' to throw you in that buggy an' chouse you out of the yard."

Doc also rose, watching the older man fighting not to show his pain. He smiled and said, "You couldn't throw a fox out of a chicken house." He held the door for Jeremiah to hitch past him into the gloomy old house, which Doc had been in before and had always thought that it was like a boar's nest, like two-thirds of the other residences he had been in around Piute Valley where single men lived. It was usually worse if they were old single men like Jeremiah Macklin.

Macklin's kitchen had one dirty window in the east wall. The sun came through only briefly during morning hours. Now it was somewhere above the ridgeline and the kitchen was gloomy. It was also none too clean, but Jeremiah had

49

steadfastly refused to hire a live-in female to care for the house and do the cooking. There were four pictures of his dead wife in the house: one on a bench beside his bed, one on the fireplace mantel in the parlor, another beside his favorite chair in the parlor, and the fourth was on a cutting table in the kitchen facing the door so that whenever Jeremiah came into the kitchen, he saw her looking at him.

She also looked at Doctor Winthrop who was also a widower. Doc had only one picture of his dead wife. It was on the mantel of his house back in town.

Jeremiah began complaining about too much rain a month or so back, and not a blessed damned drop since then. Ideally, Piute Valley needed one decent rain a month, and for some reason known only to God, or someone anyway, the few times Jeremiah could remember this happening, had also coincided with the lowest price for beef he could recall.

He also discussed what was closest to his heart — upgrading cattle, something he had inaugurated in Piute Valley twenty years earlier. But he had complaints about that too. He paid as much as two hundred cash dollars for purebred red-back bulls and they'd worked wonders on his calf crops over the years. But, the people who raised those damned short-horned, stumpy-

legged, blocky-built animals did it on soft grassland, and when the cattle were brought to Piute
Valley and turned loose to take care of Macklin
cows, they had to walk miles and miles to do
their business — and wouldn't you know it,
they didn't have the hooves for rocky ground.
"We spend a couple of days every blessed month
chousin' them out of mud holes where they go
and stand for days on end to soak the fever
out'n their feet. You know what that means,
Doc?"

"No, what?"

"A bull in a mud hole don't cover cows, that's
what it means. Barren cows don't calf, and I
got to feed them though anyway because it's
not their fault we come up with a third as many
calves as we should have. I lose money on the
feed, I lose money because I don't have as many
cattle to sell come autumn, and I'm goin' to go
bankrupt one of these days."

That last remark was too much for Doc.
Macklin was a wealthy man and everyone knew
it, so Doc said, "Where is that whisky?"

Jeremiah turned from the stove, pointing
with a long knife. "In that cupboard, top shelf.
But the water bucket's empty so you'll have to
go draw some from the well."

Doc left the bottle on the table and welcomed
the fresh, clean air out where the dug-well

51

stood. Macklin's kitchen smelled of an awful lot of meals of grease-fried meat and burned spuds, stale coffee grounds and scraped-but-not-washed cooking pans.

Doc drew water, filled the bucket, then let the rope slide through his fingers as the bail-bucket descended into the well. He leaned on the low wooden well-house and gazed pensively in the direction of town.

He and Macklin would never see eye to eye about a lot of things. Maybe a horsethief was a contemptible son of a bitch and everything else Jeremiah had suggested, but in Doc's view a murderer was worse than a horsethief.

He started for the house lugging the bucket and when he came into the kitchen to grunt the bucket atop its stand and drop the dipper into it, he saw Jeremiah watching him. Doc said, "I'm not going to say anything more."

Jeremiah looked relieved and went back to stirring frying potatoes and meat. "I'm glad of that, Doc, because it just ain't goin' to change anything...an' I value friendship above most things."

Doc saw the two cups two-thirds full of whisky and topped them off with cold water. With his back to the older man he said, "Jeremiah?"

"What?"

"It's not over. . . . Here, take this cup." Their eyes met as Macklin contradicted Doctor Winthrop.

"It *is* over. Over and done with and dang you anyway, you just said you weren't going to say—"

Doc raised his cup. "To old friends. . . . I'll tell you why it's not over. Because he's not finished. Next time maybe it'll be one of your riders. Or maybe you, yourself. Or Buck. Or someone else you know."

"Damn you, Paul Winthrop!"

"Let me finish. You're right about those horsethieves. That is indeed over. I'm willing never to mention them again, like you suggested. That's not what's bothering me. I'm worried about the next one, and the next one, and—"

Macklin roared. "There will not be another word about any of this spoke between you an' me, or so help me gawd I'll never speak to you again as long as I live. You understand me?"

Doc nodded. "I understand you, old friend." He raised his tin cup slightly. "To your health."

It seemed to choke old Macklin to return the toast but he did it. Then he turned his back on Doc and, mad as a hornet, began slamming pans around on his stove.

5

Walt Nevins beamed as his daughter wrapped the shawl around her shoulders. The marshal had just pulled up out front in Jim Danforth's best top-buggy, and his daughter looked unusually pretty this evening. Moreover, she had a brightness to her blue eyes that suggested to Walt she had a new interest in life.

Walt approved. He lightly brushed her cheek with one hand as he leaned to hold the door open. "Have a nice time, and don't worry about Jamie."

He closed the door and spied from behind a window curtain as Marshal Padgett turned the rig and headed back the way he had come before aiming northward up the coach road. Walt hiked to the kitchen for a cup of whisky and well water. He had not been convinced for many years that there were any worse judges of men than women, but this time he felt very satisfied.

Bessie looked eighteen by starlight. Her cheeks shone and the pale dress she wore heightened the impression of girlhood — slightly abundant girlhood, but still girlhood.

Jack Padgett smiled down into her lifted face. His shirt was blue, clean, and ironed. He had brushed the beaver-belly hat and had buffed his boots. His light coat was grey with four big pockets, two on each side, and it hung open to show the carved shellbelt. He said, "Fine day. How is Jamie?"

Bessie wiggled a little to get more comfortable on the horse-hair-stuffed seat and held the shawl close while she replied. "Fine. He's doing well in school." She glanced at his handsome profile, unsure why he had chosen her out of all the other girls around the valley. There was a suspicion lying low in the back of her mind. She had learned something about men since she had come back with her son to live with her father; they actually, honestly believed that a woman who had been married could not get through a full week without a man. At first she had welcomed their interest in her because after being abandoned she had desperately needed something to reaffirm her value to herself. Then she had made the discovery: They weren't courting her, they were single-minded, every one of them; some had even acted as though they were helping her overcome a desperate need. It had sickened Bessie, then it had angered and disgusted her.

That was why last night at the public corrals she had felt a wave of suspicion when the marshal had asked her to go buggy-riding with him tonight. He was so handsome and she had been so disillusioned.

But as they drove north in the warm moonlight and talked of different things, and laughed a little, he did not once offer to touch her. He did not even turn and lean as he talked to her. And there was no buggy robe.

He left the road about a mile east of town, heading past Cemetery Hill to a faintly discernible stand of trees where a seepage spring made a dark green place. She had been taken out here before and was not smiling when he pulled in and got down to drop the tether-weight, then came to her side and gallantly offered his hand. She climbed down hugging the bundle of food in its red-and-white napkin, her pretty face tipped a little, the china blue eyes as still as stones.

They went among the trees and sat down. He put his hat carefully aside and fished out a cigar, which he lighted, then he smiled and said,

"Right warm this afternoon, wasn't it?"

She nodded. It had been hot out back where she'd stirred the big iron laundry tub, feeding firewood beneath it. "Someday," she told him with a hint of grimness in her voice, "I'm going to have one of those new laundry churns that with just a little fire I'll be able to just work the plunger up and down." She suddenly looked at him, pushing past this fond hope. "I didn't see you in town today."

He considered the end of his cheroot. "No. In my trade a man's got to stay fit. I rode out a few miles and gun-practiced."

She was watching his profile as he spoke. She knew he was a dead shot because it was common knowledge around town. "I guess just about everyone does that, don't they?"

He gravely inclined his head and held the cheroot between his teeth as he leaned to get more comfortable. He did not look at her. "That's the way folks live," he replied. "If you're in my trade, Bessie, you got to be better'n average. Much better. Hickok was, so was Stoudenmire, so was Charley Wicks, the lawman who taught me the trade back in Kansas."

She put the bundle between them and opened it. "I hope the chicken's cooked right for you, Marshal."

He watched her for a moment, then finished

57

the cigar and sat up to tuck a blue bandanna inside his collar as she offered him the food. "It's bound to be if you cooked it," he told her, helping himself to a drumstick and smiling at her.

He said nothing while he ate. She spoke a little, but because he either simply nodded his head or remained silent she gave it up.

Afterward he wiped his hands carefully and tucked the bandanna away before settling back. "Did you get enough to eat?" she asked as she removed the red-and-white napkin from between them. He nodded. "Just right. It was mighty good, Bessie. . . . Charley Wicks and I went after some outlaws who'd robbed a bank in Missouri and who were goin' through Kansas on their way south. We crept up onto them in the night and they were sittin' by a fire eating fried chicken too." His blue gaze lifted to her face. "We finished the chicken."

"You arrested them, Marshal?"

"No. Charley called once and began shooting at the same time. . . . In this business a man learns all the tricks or he don't live long enough to cast much of a shadow."

She gazed at him. "How many were there — the bank robbers, I mean?"

"Two. Well, there was an In'ian too, but a man don't count them."

58

"Yes. And we ate their supper. It was a long ride back and it was a cold night." He gazed at her still face in the moonlight. "Charley got a letter from the governor praising him for keeping the law."

Bessie forced a smile. She had to believe it was as he had said; this was the way people lived. "Folks around town respect you, Marshal. Jud Pruitt was a nice man, but even my paw, who was a friend of his, said Jud spent more time playing cards than minding the law."

Jack Padgett had heard this before, several times. He picked up the hat to brush the artistically curved brim with a sleeve. "I'll tell you, Bessie. . . . There is blessed few towns in cow country who have professional lawmen; they hire someone who lives in town, someone folks like." He put the hat aside.

Bessie thought this topic had been exhausted so she switched to something else, something closer to her own interests. "You're Jamie's hero, Marshal."

He nodded. "Yes. I'm used to that."

She sat silent a moment, then said, "When you fixed his wagon after the stage ran over it. . .folks liked that. . .and so did I."

"It goes with the badge, Bessie."

She thought about that and decided he was correct because old Jud had done things like that when he hadn't been busy. She started the conversation on an even more personal route.

"I was married, you know, and...he just rode off one day with some of his friends."

"So I've heard."

"Well, wouldn't you think a man's son would mean more to him than that even if his wife didn't?"

"Bad blood, Bessie. Lots of men got it. His name was Dick Arnett wasn't it?"

"Yes."

Marshal Padgett looked casually upward at the rash of stars. "I heard that was his name. Out of Wyoming was he?"

"Yes. That's where he grew up. Near Fort Laramie. He started riding up there....We went back up there...and he...just rode away one day." Bessie had to lock her jaw for a moment and blink away the sudden scald of tears. She said, "Were you ever married, Marshal?"

"No ma'am. In my trade a man's better off not to be."

She nodded about that; he did not want to leave a widow behind to mourn. It was a considerate way to be.

"A man has to move around a lot, Bessie, and he can't be fettered."

Her eyes came up slowly. "Well, if you found the right woman, Marshal," she murmured,

60

and under the guise of straightening her skirt eased over a little closer to him. "Isn't it a beautiful night...Jack?"

"It is for a fact. Summer's here now. It makes the ground too hard for tracking, but I expect a man can't have everything, can he?"

She smiled up into his face. "Maybe not everything, but enough — maybe — Jack."

He met her china blue gaze. "Tell me about Arnett, Bessie. Did he run much with a wild bunch?"

Her gaze changed a little. "Well, maybe no more than most rangemen are wild." She eased back and drew up her legs to encircle both knees with her arms and stare straight ahead.

"Never in trouble with the law was he?"

She shook her head. "No....A woman up there told me that lots of cowboys are like that....Never really grow up."

He watched her profile for a moment then spoke again. "They grow up all right, Bessie. Men who wear six-shooters are grown up." He looked at the sky again. "I expect the cattlemen are cryin' for rain."

She turned very slowly and looked at him. Then she seemingly without any intention to do so brushed his arm with her hand, and when he turned she smiled directly into his eyes.

Padgett brought forth another cheroot and

lit it, then leaned back in the grass. "Your paw's store does quite a business. I've sat over in my office watchin' folks go in and out." He blew smoke at the sky. "That old safe he's got wouldn't stand up under a stick of dynamite. He'd ought to get a bigger and better one."

Bessie was expressionless for a moment, then leaned and said, "It's such a beautiful night. Warm and fragrant and all," then she emulated him by lying back in the grass, softly smiling.

His gaze drifted from her face to the buggy and the drowsing horse between the shafts. "Must be gettin' along toward ten o'clock," he said casually, then he faced her again and softly smiled.

She waited, scarcely breathing.

He drew the tight black gloves from under his shellbelt and slowly pulled them on. "You're a mighty fine cook. I'd say that was about as good fried chicken as I ever ate. . . . I expect we'd better be gettin' back." He stood up and held one black-gloved hand to her. She reached for it and he pulled her gently to her feet. She stood utterly still looking at him. "I'll bring the rig closer," he said, moving away. Her eyes did not leave him and her expression did not change, but she was pale and did not seem to even be breathing as he led the mare over and offered her his hand again. She climbed in, waited for him to get settled at her side with the lines in his hands, then she turned and looked hard at him again.

He made several casual attempts to start a conversation on the ride back but she was quiet. He looked around a couple of times, then allowed the silence to last until they drew to a halt outside of her house and he came around to offer his hand again.

She climbed down by herself, hurt and humiliation bright in her glance at him. He smiled and held the gate for her, then strode as far as the porch before speaking. "It was right nice, Bessie."

She waited. He nodded and turned his back heading out through the gate to the rig. She remained motionless watching him talk up the horse and make a complete turn heading back toward Main Street. She was still standing like that after he had passed from her sight when Walt came out onto the porch to say, "I'll bet he liked that fried chicken, didn't he?"

She faced around slowly. "Is Jamie asleep, Pa?"

"Yes. Never made a sound."

She walked past him into the house and went to her room, leaving Walt in the doorway staring after her. He heard the door close behind her, got untracked and went as far as his favorite chair where he'd been sitting with the lamp turned down waiting for her return, with a glass of watered whisky for company.

6

She dutifully made her father's breakfast the following morning but when he entered the kitchen she was not there, nor did she appear even after he had finished and was ready to head for the store.

He did not really look for her, but he called her name a couple of times before putting on his hat and leaving the house.

There was something wrong, he knew that, had known it last night the way she had refused to even speak to him and had gone straight to her room.

Walt's clerk, an old man who also wore black cotton sleeve-protectors and was as thin and juiceless as a stone, helped Walt take the cash from the safe and count it into the money drawers, a ritual they had been observing for fifteen years each weekday morning before unlocking the roadway doors for business.

This morning the old man had corrected Walt twice when he miscounted the money. The third time he did that the old man said nothing, just stared at him from slightly protruding wet grey eyes.

Later, during a lull, the old man happened to be nearby and said, "Somethin' troubling you, Mister Nevins?"

Walt's knitted brows cleared briefly. "Bothering me? Why should anything be bothering me, Angus? Look out that window, fine day, not a cloud in sight."

The old man shuffled away as two women entered carrying net bags on their arms, and Walt automatically nodded as they went past, then leaned on the counter looking through his front-wall window in the direction of the jailhouse. Marshal Padgett was standing out front talking to a man named Buff Conley who had a small ranch south of town.

Three faded rangemen entered the store. They were beard-stubbled and leathery-faced individuals. Three sets of hard eyes measured Walt as they walked to his counter and asked for three sacks of Durham smoking tobacco. While he was reaching into the carton with the picture of a big angry bull on its side, the rangemen stood hipshot, thumbs hooked in shell-belts, gazing around the store. When Walt put the sacks down one of the leathery-faced men smiled at him.

"Mighty pretty town," he remarked, counting out the silver and handing it over.

Walt agreed. "I've been in worse towns."

"Busy too," said the cowboy, handing the sacks around among his companions and pocketing one for himself. "I never been up here before. Piute Valley, ain't it?"

There were no other customers for the moment and Angus was helping the women, so Walt leaned on the counter as he replied. "Yes, it's called Piute Valley. Used to be a trading post and camp for hide hunters. I wasn't around then, but that's the story I've always heard. . . . Yes, it gets along for a fact." Walt eyed the trio. "You boys passing through?"

The spokesman smiled. "Yeah. It's likely too late to get hired on."

That was true enough. "I'd guess so. Spring comes early up here, most of the time anyway, and the ranches hire on early so's they can get it all done before autumn."

The cowboy kept smiling. "I'm right obliged," he said and led his companions back out into the roadway.

Across the road and up a couple of doors Marshal Padgett and Buff Conley were ending

67

their discussion. Buff walked down in the direction of Danforth's barn.

One of the lanky, faded cowboys lifted his eyes from rolling a cigarette and quietly said, "Look yonder. I'll bet he's never even had no sweat inside his hat." He licked the paper, completed the roll, and struck a match that sputtered violently and gave off a fist-sized cloud of sulphur smoke. The man smiled coldly through smoke. "I seen a picture of one like him years back in a magazine."

Another rangeman picked it up sounding even more contemptuous. "Pretty as one of them Colt repeating firearms ads."

They ambled south and Marshal Padgett crossed on a diagonal course toward the cafe, heading north.

Doctor Winthrop was having breakfast when the marshal sat down beside him and nodded. "Good morning. Is that good sausage, Doc?"

It was. "Try it, Marshal. A little spicy but that's how I like sausage."

Padgett gave his order to the cafeman and tipped back his hat. It was going to be hot today. His coffee arrived first, but it was too hot to drink so the marshal glanced around. There was only one other diner besides Doctor Winthrop. It was Don Myser, the town blacksmith. They exchanged a nod; Don was serious about eating and rarely tried to carry on a conversation at the same time.

When the food arrived Marshal Padgett went to work. Doc had finished eating and held up his cup for a refill. Then he nursed the cup with both hands and watched Marshal Padgett eat.

Out of a clear blue sky he said, "Did you put in for the bounty on those four horsethieves, Marshal?"

Padgett bobbed his head and continued to eat.

Doc tried the coffee; it was still hot but drinkable. "There aren't any names on their headboards," he said, almost as though he were speaking to himself.

Padgett was between mouthfuls and turned his head. "Horse thief is good enough, Doctor. I've been in towns where they wouldn't even allow horsethieves to be buried alongside decent folks."

Doc paid up and walked outside. It was not hot yet but it was going to be. He idly watched three lanky rangeriders sit down upon the old bench outside Sam Starr's harness works, then headed toward his house. The three front rooms had been used as his working area for many years. The room closest to his kitchen, which was at the back of the house, Doc used for anyone he had to put to bed. That way it was easier to feed them.

He had no appointments today, but then he rarely had appointments anyway. People just rode in, or they walked over from around town. Yesterday he had been napping out back in the shade when a woman had brought in her kid who had fallen from an apple tree. He'd broken his right arm, and once the pain and fear were past after Doc splinted the limb, the boy raised his freckled face and grinned at Doc, "No sense in goin' to school," he had said, "when I can't write."

Doc could have told him differently; he knew the lad's mother. She had taken him by the ear and led him out of the house telling him bleakly that both George Washington and Abraham Lincoln had been left-handed.

Doc did a lot of things for himself, including his own house cleaning. He balked at doing laundry or washing windows, but he wielded a mean broom when he was in the mood for it.

He was raising dust with a cud of Kentucky twist in his cheek when the Patterson ranch wagon pulled up out front and the driver got down to help a man lying on straw in the back to get onto his feet. Doc saw this through the window, leaned aside his broom, and went to hold the door for them. He did not know either of them, but he rarely sorted out faces among rangeriders who were usually only seasonal

70

employees anyway. However, he knew the Patterson wagon. Anyone would have who also knew the Patterson brand because it had been burned into the wagon on both sides, just below the spring-seat.

The uninjured cowboy helped his companion to a chair and blew out a big breath as he faced Doc. "We figured at the ranch it's a busted leg, Doctor. Horse jumped him off going through the corral gate and kicked as he went down. Caught him pretty high up on the left leg. . . . You know Burt Standish?"

"Yes."

"Well sir, he sent me in and said for me to tell you he'd pay the bill." As the rider got all this out, he looked around at the younger, tousle-headed man on the bench whose face was white and whose teeth were clenched. "His name's Whitey Ford. . . . I'll come back in an hour or so."

Doctor Winthrop nodded, turned his back on the healthy one, and prodded the unhealthy one to his feet, supporting him as he hopped into the examination room. When the cowboy was lying back Doc removed his britches before beginning his examination. He went to a window to spray tobacco juice into the geranium bed below, then returned to the cowboy and said, "Clean break, son. You're lucky; I've had

71

'em in here with splintered bones that never heal right. This one will be just fine, but you'll be on the ground with crutches for a while."

Whitey Ford had sweat on his upper lip. "How long?" he asked.

Doc was picking among the whittled splints he kept in a tall brass cane rack as he answered. "About three months — if you don't do something that'll part the bone ends again. An extra month for good measure wouldn't hurt." Doc returned with the two splints and eyed the cowboy. He had peach fuzz instead of whiskers on his face. "How old are you?'

Whitey was apprehensive about Doc, the sticks he was holding, and not being able to work for three or four months. He said, "I'm twenty. . . . You got anything I can drink before you set to work?"

Doc ignored the question and considered the sweaty face. "If you're twenty, son, I'm fifteen. Care to try again?"

Whitey's pain was less now than it had been since early morning. Now there was shock and demoralization as he leaned his head flat down and stared upward. "Comin' eighteen," he said. "Maybe there's someone around who could go over to the saloon, Doctor."

Doc snorted. "It'll hurt only for a minute. After that you'll feel almost as good as new.

72

Now then — take hold of the sides of the table, boy, and don't move that leg. . . . You ready?" Doc pulled in both directions, the cowboy was grinding his teeth. Doc said, "Stop that. I'm listenin' for the bone ends to mesh. Just be quiet."

They meshed and Doc cautioned Whitey again about not moving even his little toe. Water was running off the cowboy's face as Doc began splinting and bandaging the leg. He said, "How long you worked for Patterson ranch?" in an attempt to keep the cowboy's mind off his injury. At seventeen going on eighteen sometimes they weren't any different from ten-year-olds going on eleven.

"Since March. . . . That son of a bitching horse!"

"Been workin' for 'em since March? Burt's a good man. You could have done a lot worse." Doc stopped moving and slowly raised his eyes to the cowboy's face. He remained like that for a moment, then resumed his bandaging. When he was finished he said, "Lie still. I'll be back directly," and went to the kitchen, tumbled whisky and water into a cup, and brought it back. "Sit up. I'll hold an arm behind you — but don't move that damned leg. You ready now?"

Whitey Ford took the cup and drank it empty,

73

then Doc eased him back down very gently and put the cup aside, went to the window to jettison his cud, and returned to study the cowboy's pale features. Gradually, they were getting good color.

Doc said, "That was one hell of a shoot-out, wasn't it?"

The youth's eyes swung to Doc's face and remained there.

Doc smiled and wagged his head as he moved down a little to probe the bandage. "I heard all about it....Marshal Padgett chargin' right down their gunbarrels."

Whitey's eyes did not leave Doc's face. "Who told you?"

Doc was leaning, examining his bandaging job with what seemed to be total concentration. And he lied. "Mister Macklin told me.... Shot that one in the back who was trying to get away and..."

Whitey let his head back down on the table very gently and stared at the ceiling. "And the other one," he half whispered.

Doc raised up looking at the cowboy's face. "Yes, and that one too. The only one left."

"Right in the face...God a'mighty. Right in the face with him holding both arms in the air."

Doctor Winthrop fished for his tobacco and settled a fresh cud inside his cheek. He returned

74

to the window and stood there a long time before going back where he could look down into the cowboy's face. "With his arms up trying to surrender?"

"Yes," the youth whispered, and Doc touched his shoulder lightly. "What'd your friend say your name was?"

"Whitey Ford."

"Listen to me, Whitey. Don't tell anyone you told me anything, because — it'll be best for you not to mention it. Not even to Burt. You understand?"

The blue eyes rolled to Doc's face. "You already knew."

"All the same, son, not a single word. Something like this a man don't even *think* about let alone talk about. Not even among friends."

Whitey's eyes were fixed on Doc. "Not even think about it! You ever seen a man shot down like that? How does a man keep from thinking about it?" The whisky had brought full color back to Whitey's face and along with it something else — crawling nerves. "That's what Mister Macklin said — we was to forget we ever seen it. Then he went and told you."

"That don't matter, Whitey. Not where you are concerned. Do you understand me?"

"Yeah, I understand you." Whitey was silent for a moment. "I'll tell you what I think I'll do, draw my pay and get out of this country. Hell, I was lookin' for work when I come here and I'll be lookin' for work when I leave here."

"Where are you from?"

"Omaha. I was in an orphanage back there. I run away two years ago."

Doc heard bootsteps on his outside porch. The other rider was probably returning. He lay a hand lightly on Whitey's shoulder. "Keep off this leg for at least two months, three if you can and even four months."

"Yeah, sit in front of the barn in the sun and expect them to pay me," the youngster said bitterly.

"I told you, Burt's a good man. It wasn't your fault anyway." Doc eased a hand under the cowboy's shoulders. "Sit up now. Good. Now then, lean on me and don't put the busted leg to the ground. Lean...slow now."

They made it out to the waiting room where the other rangerider watched their progress in silence until Doc beckoned to him and eased the burden from his own shoulders to the younger man's. He repeated to the uninjured cowboy what he had cautioned Whitey about. "No riding, no walking, not even any wagon driving for two or three months. He's young so the bone'll mend fast. But he's got to be careful. If he breaks it in the same place again he'll likely end up walking with a limp for the rest of his life. You tell Burt I said that, will you?"

Doc helped them out to the porch and down the walkway, out the gate and up onto the wagon seat. He stood watching them drive away. As he was turning slowly to go back to the house he saw Marshal Padgett talking to Arley Patton in front of the saloon, and he stood for a long time gazing at the handsome lawman. Three trail-stained lanky rangeriders were crossing the road from in front of Sam Starr's shop in the direction of the cafe, but Doc no more than glanced in their direction.

Doc eventually returned to the house to clean up his room and take the cup out to the kitchen. While still holding it, he lifted the whisky bottle, splashed the cup one-third full, and watered it from the bucket near the stove. Then he went out back where the birds were making a racket in one of his trees and stood in the house shade sipping whisky.

He let go with a big, ragged breath, tossed what little whisky was in the bottom of his cup into the weeds, and raised his eyes. There were some sheep clouds up there in rows. Sometimes that meant rain was on the way. Other times it did not mean a damned thing.

Doc returned to the house.

7

Jim Danforth told his daymen in a sour moment that the three horses those rough-looking, down-at-the-heel strangers had left at the barn had to be stolen because they were part thorough-bred; fine animals of the kind that ordinarily cost a lot of money and those three saddle tramps never in their lives would have the kind of money it took to buy such horses.

The dayman's reaction was as it usually was when Jim was in an evil mood — he nodded his head, kept his mouth closed, and escaped from his employer's company as quickly as he could.

What had occasioned Danforth's spite had been a request the evening before by one of those strangers that he take all three animals over to Myser's shop and have them freshly shod all around.

Don greeted the liveryman with a curt nod

78

and a jerk of his head. "Tie 'em out back in the shade, Jim. I got three tires to sweat onto wheels for the stage company first. Get to 'em when I can." As Danforth went past, leading the horses, Don Myser straightened up from his forge. "Whose animals are they?" he asked.

Danforth did not stop walking. "Some fellers who come into town yesterday. . . . Saddle tramps from the looks of 'em."

Don went back to work with a parting observation. "For saddle tramps they ride mighty fine horses." He sounded skeptical of Danforth's judgment.

Jeremiah Macklin hauled up out front in an old battered spring wagon and shouted until Don walked out front, wiping both hands on a dirty rag and looking annoyed. Jeremiah got carefully down and pointed to the underside of his light rig. "One of those guide rods busted when I was tryin' to miss a big boulder, and hit another one I didn't even see." His squinty eyes went to Myser's face. "I'll only be in town long enough to get the mail and a few supplies and see Doc. How soon can you fix it?"

Don continued to dry his large hands, knowing very well that if he mentioned having to sweat tires to wheels and then shoe three horses old Macklin would have a fit, so he said, "Directly. Depends on what I run into under there."

Jeremiah was turning when he said, "I'll take it kindly, Mister Myser."

Don watched Macklin go hobbling in the direction of the store. He returned to his forge as Jim Danforth was returning from out back. Jim saw the old spring wagon out front and said, "Macklin?"

"Yeah. Hit a rock and broke something beneath his wagon. He favors when he walks. I never noticed that before."

Danforth's sour expression had not changed. "What do you expect from a feller into his eighties?"

Don frowned. "He's not that old, Jim. Maybe seventy but not much more."

Danforth glared at the blacksmith and walked out into the roadway on his way over to the barn. He met those three strangers in the runway talking to his dayman and curtly nodded as he headed for the harness room. One of the lanky men halted him. "We was just wonderin' if you took the horses over to be shod."

Danforth eyed them distastefully. For one thing his mood was bad, for another thing he did not like cowboys and never had. "Just this minute come back," he stated. "The blacksmith said he'll have 'em finished directly."

Another man spoke sharply. "What does directly mean?"

Jim shrugged heavy shoulders. "It means when he gets finished with some wheels for the corralyard folks, he'll get onto your animals. I'd guess he'll have 'em finished by noon. You fellers in a hurry?"

The man who had spoken fixed Jim Danforth with a steely look. "Just wanted to know is all, mister. . . . You get up on the wrong side of the bed this morning?"

Jim Danforth's mind was shrilling a soundless alarm. He considered the trio, then forced a smile and said, "Ate somethin' last night that didn't set well. I'll bring the horses back as soon as the smith's finished with 'em." He ducked for his harness room.

Myser had to send his helper up to Nevins' store for some flux, otherwise he could not finish the stagecoach wheels — the tires actually. As Walt got it for him and made a notation that Don owed him because the swamper had no money, Jeremiah Macklin hobbled in.

He handed Walt Nevins a crumpled scrap of brown paper. "Set that stuff out for me. I'll be back directly. Got to see Doc. And set the mail out for me too."

Nevins nodded and watched old Macklin leave the store thinking that, finally, age was overtaking the indestructible old cowman.

Doc did not think this when Jeremiah banged

on his front door. In fact Doc acted slightly un-
nerved to see Macklin standing there when he
opened the door and stepped aside.

Without a greeting Macklin skewered Doc
with a flinty look and said, "That medicine
didn't do me one bit of good. Not only that but
the confounded leg is gettin' worse."

Doc led the way to his examination room
and motioned for Jeremiah to sit on the table.
Doc probed, tested reflexes, and poked a stiff
thumb into the older man's thigh. When Jeremiah resoundingly swore, Doc stepped back,
looking at him. "It wasn't that sore a couple of
days ago," he said.

Macklin glared. "Well, it is now."

"What have you been doing?"

"Doing?" sputtered the cowman. "What does
a man usually do when he runs a cow outfit?
We have to move cattle and—"

"Jeremiah, I told you—"

"Paul, you told me to stay out'n the cold, and
that's what I been doing because it hasn't been
under eighty degrees in a week."

"And," stated Doc evenly, "stop riding horses,
stop walking a lot — stop using that damned
leg. Favor it."

"That's all you can tell me?"

Doc smiled a little. "I'm a physician not a
magician. That's all I can tell you. It's the Lum-

bago in your hip joint, Jeremiah. You've been fighting all your life. What the hell are you fighting now? There's no enemy left, you've either whipped them or they've died off. Indians, rustlers, renegades, drought....But you're still fighting. It's become your nature. Only now it's shadows."

Doc turned to lead the way into an untidy book-filled room. He poured some liquid from a large blue bottle into a smaller one and handed the little bottle to Jeremiah. "This stuff'll stop the pain."

Macklin, looking skeptical, held the blue bottle in a scarred, callused hand. "That's what you said about the other medicine."

"This," stated Doc, "is laudanum. Listen to me. It will stop the pain. But if you think that just because you don't feel anything the hip socket is all right, and you go riding around or working hard, the joint will likely deteriorate. Are you listening?"

"Well for Chris'sake yes, I'm listening. That's all I've had a chance to do since I—"

"Jeremiah, if you think it's painful now, you abuse it to the point of skeletal deterioration and the pain you've had up to now will seem like a Sunday school picnic. Only use that stuff when you have to. You owe me two dollars."

Macklin started, his sore leg touched the

floor, he swore and shifted his weight, then he said, "Two dollars? Paul Winthrop, you are a bigger bandit than Jesse James ever thought of being."

"Two dollars," stated Doc in an unyielding voice.

Macklin dug deep and brought forth two silver cartwheels. "An' that wasn't even decent malt whisky, you confounded old highbinder."

Doc pocketed the money. "You took up most of my morning. It's close to noon....And the reason I don't drink malt whisky is because with skinflints for patients, I can't afford it."

They returned through the house to the parlor where old Macklin retrieved his hat, pocketed the little bottle, and eyed his old friend. "What's making you so ornery?"

Doc faced him. "You ought to know. Anyhow you said you didn't want to hear it."

"I never said any such a damned thing. I said I never wanted to *talk* about that again. Well, it's the truth. I don't, only I know you and when you get that miserable hang-dog look on your face....Go ahead, I'm listening."

"Marshal Padgett shot one of them in the back when the man was running away and he shot the last one of them in the head when he was standing up without a gun, with both hands over his head."

It was so quiet in the parlor that Don Myser, at the lower end of town shaping steel over his anvil, made a clarion ring that sounded very close.

Jeremiah stared for a long time before speaking. One thing he had learned down the years was that when Doc looked the way he was looking now, he knew what he was talking about. He let his breath out. "Who told you that, Paul?"

"When we were in your kitchen I said—"

"Naw. You were guessing then, Paul. Right now you're not guessing. Who told you?"

"It's the truth, isn't it? And you told them as the smoke was lifting to never say a word about what they had seen."

"Damn flannelmouths," Macklin growled, looking for a place to sit because the hip was bothering him. "You're not going to tell me his name are you?"

Doc waited to reply until his friend was seated. "No. That don't matter anyway. What matters is what happened out there. Jeremiah, a horsethief bad as he is, can't hold a candle to a murderer."

Macklin had his head back and slightly to one side. He was studying Doctor Winthrop with a tough, skeptical look. He remained silent for a long while.

"Did you know I had a son, Doc?"

Winthrop blinked. It was not a statement he could have anticipated.

"That rider of mine they call Mitch. Mitchell Smith. You know him?"

Doc nodded. He actually only knew Mitch Smith because he had been working year-round for Macklin since Doc had arrived to settle in Piute Valley. He had spoken to Smith a few times, casually around town or at Arley's place. He had heard Smith was old Macklin's top-hand, was a good man with livestock, and that was about all Doc knew of the man.

"Y' see, Doc? I've been in this valley more years than you have lived and no one ever knew that until right this minute. What I'm saying is that there are some things a man just never opens his mouth about. Padgett shot those two in cold blood. Nothing is goin' to bring them back. Besides, they were worthless, horse stealing sons of bitches. You're plumb right, it was murder. Now what good is it goin' to do to tell that around? No good at all, and it will sure as hell get you killed for saying it. I know men like Jack Padgett. Want to know how I figured them over seventy years of knowing them?"

Doc nodded woodenly.

"They got straw inside and cold water for blood. Somethin' was left out when they was made. They are specialists in just one thing

86

and got no feeling about anything else. They live it, Doc, and they'll die it — first-rate killers who see themselves as gawd-appointed executioners. They dress the part, look the part, and Doc, they aren't acting because that's what they are through and through."

As the silence returned between them there was a thunderous explosion somewhere near the lower middle section of town. Doc's house shuddered and old Macklin tried to spring to his feet.

Doc was stunned but he reacted by whirling toward the front door.

8

Jeremiah Macklin did not reach the front porch until Doc was already out by the gate. Macklin called breathlessly. "What was it?"

Doc was staring southward and only shook his head to indicate that he did not know.

There was something that seemed a cross between smoke and dust pouring from the doorway of Nevins' general store. One of those lanky strangers was across the road in front of Sam Starr's harness works at the hitch-rack where three frightened horses were pulling back and lunging. The lanky man was swearing at them but his face was turned toward the general store.

Macklin hobbled out where Doc was standing as two fast gunshots erupted, sounding muffled. Then there was a third gunshot, and two men came running through the smoke and dust heading toward the three horses and the man with them across the road. Macklin yelped, "Robbery, Paul. For Chris'sake it's Walt's store!" He almost bowled Doc over as he lunged past, out through the gate, drawing his old Colt as he went rushing like a crab, as much sideways as forward, in the direction of the harness shop.

The three lanky men were fighting their horses around, freed of the rack, to get astride, something they could have accomplished better if they had not been gripping six-guns and little flour sacks in their hands.

Two men burst forth from Arley Patton's saloon. One was Don Myser, the other was Marshal Padgett.

Old Macklin roared at the three mounting men and paused to raise his six-gun. One of the mounted men twisted, aimed and fired. Jeremiah's weapon discharged into the plank-walk as he was going down.

Another of the horsemen fired three times very fast in the direction of the saloon. Marshal Padgett drew and fired back with incredible speed, but the horsemen had their spurs hung into rib bones, their reins flopping. The horses, hot-blooded and already terrified, broke clear and landed hard down in a flat race toward the lower end of town.

Padgett walked to the middle of the road and

fired again. Two of the mounted men twisted and emptied their guns. Arley Patton had just come past his spindle doors carrying a shotgun. He didn't make a sound, he simply settled both shoulders against the rough exterior siding of his saloon and dropped the scattergun.

Marshal Padgett started walking down the center of the roadway, firing at the fleeing horsemen who were crouching over their saddlehorns as they raced past Danforth's barn. Jim's dayman, who had been peering out, turned to flee down the runway. One bullet between the shoulder blades put him down in a flinging sprawl.

Danforth rushed out of the harness room and stopped dead in his tracks. By the time he raised his head from the dead body, the horsemen were out of sight and on their way southward. Only a little sift of rising roadway dust showed that they had passed his barn doorway.

Marshal Padgett came up in a run and told Jim to saddle his horse, then the Lawman stood in the barn doorway methodically shucking out casings and plugging in fresh loads from his shellbelt. When the weapon was ready he dropped it into the carved leather holster and stood facing where dust showed the route of the fleeing men.

There were still echoes when Danforth

handed Marshal Padgett the reins and spoke from a white face. "Gawda'mighty what did they do?" and before Padgett could have answered, although obviously he was not going to as he swung over leather and hauled his horse around southward, Jim said, "I'll get some men," and went running clumsily up toward the middle of town.

Doc heard someone yelling his name and ignored it as he started walking down the plankwalk to where Jeremiah was lying.

Danforth got up as far as the general store, then seemed to forget his mission as he leaned to look inside. With both hands he reached for support on the doorjamb.

A cyclone could not have caused more damage. The explosion, which had blown the little steel safe off the floor and through the dry goods counter, leaving it doorless and cracked from top to bottom, had also hurled bolt goods, groceries, even a coal oil barrel from shelves and stands into the middle of the big old room. The dust was chokingly thick. The place was a shambles with leaking coal oil adding to the smell of burnt powder and bursted tins of everything from corn to black strap molasses.

Jim had the presence of mind to go inside, making his way through the devastation to the coal oil barrel, and tip it upright so that it no

91

longer leaked. Then on his way out, he encountered someone he could not see very well through watering eyes and yelled at him. "Stand in the door. Don't let nobody in. There's coal oil all over the floor. If it catches fire the whole damn town'll burn up."

He paused to cough and rub his eyes then pressed onward in the direction of the saloon — the only place, it had occurred to him, he might find enough men to go after the strangers who had dynamited Walt's safe and robbed his cash drawers.

In front of the spindle doors Don Myser was lying on his face with one arm crooked beneath him. Blood had stopped running from his mouth and nose. He was dead. Ten feet away sitting completely relaxed, legs outstretched, back against the wall, a shotgun lying nearby, Arley Patton was leaning slightly, his head hanging. A small ring of scarlet brightened the very center of his shirt. He, too, was dead.

Jim Danforth had exhausted his initial thrust. He went to the edge of the plankwalk and slowly sat down, looking dumbly over toward Starr's saddle shop where Doctor Winthrop and the old rugged-faced harness maker were kneeling beside Jeremiah Macklin. There was blood over there too, but not as much.

Danforth turned his head very slowly in

response to someone's outcry from down in front of the general store. People had begun to emerge from buildings and cautiously sidle in that direction, evidently attracted by the smoke and dust which was still drifting lazily.

Several men pushed inside. Another man protested and tried to keep the others out by yelling something about coal oil. Danforth lowered his head slowly and placed both hands over his face as though to shut out the world.

Doctor Winthrop saw him sitting over there and dispatched the harness maker to see if Jim had been shot. He then looked down at the grey face in front of him and said, "Be still." He had already cut through cloth to expose the bullet wound and now, with a wooden expression, he went to work on it.

When the harness maker returned, Doc told him to stay with Macklin, not to let him move, and ran to his house for his medicine bag and some other things. By the time he got back to Macklin, the town was in an uproar. People were acting like sheep, except for four or five men who were running toward Danforth's barn with guns in their hands.

There was a body on the plankwalk out front of Nevin's store that someone had covered with a clean grey blanket, probably brought from out of the store.

Doctor Winthrop raised his head, listened to the commotion out front of the general store, and told the harness maker to go down there; that if indeed there was coal oil the harness maker had better keep everyone out, especially anyone who might be smoking. After the harness maker had gone Doc went back to work. He did not meet the wide-open eyes looking up at him, but he said, "Just be still, Jeremiah."

With a flash of his natural temperament old Macklin said, "Where the hell do you think I'm going? Where did the son of a bitch hit me? I can't feel anything."

Doc held up the empty little blue bottle. "That's why you can't feel anything."

"Where did he hit me?"

"Shut up and lie still," Doc replied, working expertly.

Juniper had never seen such confusion, chaos and disorder even when it had been a trading post with redskins trying to burn it out and massacre everyone. But no one living there now knew anything about those earlier times, and right now they would not have cared if they had known.

Doc tried without success to hail some men to help him carry old Macklin up to his house. Jim Danforth raised his head, looked over there, then rose and walked heavily across the road.

Without a word he leaned to join Doc in carrying Jeremiah up to the house. Afterward Danforth returned as far as Doc's waiting room and sat in a chair out there until the afternoon was advancing. When he finally rose and departed, he walked southward toward his barn without speaking to anyone or even seeming to have seen anyone.

By late afternoon moccasin telegraph had reached Patterson ranch, and Burt Standish with his remaining three rangemen loped into town armed to the teeth. The fourth rider had drawn his pay, had straddled his personal horse with his splinted leg shoved through a blanket-sling secured to the horn, and had ridden northward on his way out of the country.

Jeremiah was lying in a room of the Winthrop house when Burt walked up to the porch and rattled the front door with a gloved fist.

Doc opened it without nodding or speaking. His embalming shed was across the alley and he had just come from there, leaving a number of still, silent people hovering outside in the alley with failing daylight mantling them.

Burt said, "What happened?"

Doc did not move out of the opening. "Three men blew Nevin's safe with dynamite and made off with whatever was in the thing."

"Where is Marshal Padgett?"

"He went after them."

"Alone?"

"I don't know. I think so."

Burt swung a hawkish profile to look down the empty, silent roadway. "Which way?"

"South. . . . Someone said three or four men from town went after them, behind Marshal Padgett."

Burt started to turn before speaking again. "Anyone hurt, Doc?"

"We can talk when you get back," Winthrop replied and closed the door.

Nobody had been hurt as far as Doc knew now, excepting Jeremiah Macklin, but he had four dead bodies out in his shed across the alley. Don Myser, the blacksmith, Arley Patton the saloonman, old Angus the clerk at Nevin's store, who had been nearly cut in two when that dynamited safe had struck him, and Danforth's hostler. But as Doc made his way back in the direction of the alley he did not believe the total carnage had been tallied, and he was right. Just before nightfall four men carrying something in an old army blanket brought in the cafeman. He had taken a handgun bullet through the head. How this had happened no one knew, and in fact no one ever would know, but it was later on generally accepted that he had tried to flee from his cafe after the explosion, which was only a couple of doors from his cafe, and had probably got no farther than the doorway when someone had knocked him backward with a bullet through the brain.

Doc shooed away the leaden-faced people in the back alley and told them to go home – go some place anyway. He then went inside, lighted the old lamp and, before starting to clean up the bodies and make them as presentable as possible, he leaned on the wall looking among them. He had known every one of them, Danforth's hostler least of all, but he had even known him from thanking the man for harnessing up the buggy when Doc'd had emergency calls beyond town.

As his eyes settled upon Angus, the old store clerk, he got a jolt. Walt sure as hell had also been in the store; then where was he now?

The rugged-faced old harness maker came knocking on the door. When Doc opened it the big old rawboned man solemnly asked if Doc needed any help. He was, he said, experienced at sewing things up.

Doc shook his head. "No thanks, Sam. But there is something you can do: See if you can find Walt Nevins. He had to be in there when they blew open the safe."

The harness maker nodded and walked away.

Formaldehyde had a bad scent even when someone was accustomed to it. Doc did not use it, but he had used it many times in this little old converted carriage house and the smell must have penetrated the dry wood. Even on nice summer days when he'd left the alleyway door open to air the place out, the smell had remained.

He was not going to have to embalm anyone this evening. Not tomorrow either. Swen would get the coffins finished as rapidly as possible, and the town would hold a funeral out at Cemetery Hill, and there would be a burial. Anyway, with someone like old Angus there was no way to do an embalming job.

Doc went after a fresh bucket of water in his well behind the house and returned to finish up. He pouched a cud into his cheek and worked methodically, thinking back to incidents from his life which had included every one of these men. It was easy to be a professional when a man didn't know victims as well as Doc had known each of these people.

Later, he blew down the mantle of the lamp and locked the shed from the outside, crossing to his kitchen for a splash of whisky and water in a crockery cup. He wrinkled his nose, because the aroma of formaldehyde clung to him as it always did when he'd been over there very long, then he put aside the empty cup, and considered the closed door of Jeremiah's room.

That Laudanum would not last forever. He picked up the whisky bottle, the crockery cup, and went over to the door.

He was going to lose another friend. Maybe they could have a drink first.

9

Walt Nevins appeared in Doc's doorway still wearing an expression of dumb shock, and when Doc admitted him to the parlor Walt said, "Is my clerk out back? Someone told me he was."

Doc nodded, eyeing the storekeeper with a professional look. "He's out there. Are you all right, Walt?"

"Yes."

"You weren't in the store?"

"No. I was across the road in the jailhouse office. There was something I'd had on my mind since last night, so I finally decided to go over and talk to Marshal Padgett."

"Was he there?"

"No. The place was empty — then the dynamite went off. I got to the doorway. It looked like my store was full of smoke." Walt sought a chair. "Marshal Padgett was standin' out front of the saloon....Everybody seemed to be firing guns. There were those three range-riders who'd been hangin' around town.... They got a-horseback....I saw one look at me and I jumped away from the door. He fired anyway. The bullet broke the lamp....I went home."

Doc did not believe he would have gone home but people react differently. Walt asked if he could see his clerk and Doc hung fire before replying. Angus looked like he'd been run through a meat grinder. "Maybe tomorrow, Walt, when Swen brings up the coffins." He changed the subject. "How much money did they get from the store?"

Walt looked blank for a moment before answering. "I don't know. I think we had about six hundred dollars on hand....I don't know. How was Angus killed, Doc?"

"He got hit by the safe when it blew up. I'd guess he didn't have any time to realize what was happening. He'd been with you a long time, eh?"

Nevins nodded, saw the closed door, and tilted his head in that direction. "Who's in there?"

"Jeremiah Macklin."

":...I had some supplies set out for him. Is he bad off, Doc?"

101

"He's dead. Walt, go on home. . . . Well, maybe you'd ought to nail some planks over the doorway of the store, then you'd better go home."

Nevins departed, moving like a man in a trance. He was not the only one in Juniper this night, and it began to lightly rain about ten o'clock, making a sound like soft tears falling.

It was not going to be much of a rainfall: These light summer rains never amounted to much except that they settled dust, softened the ground, brought a fresh cleanness to the air, and improved visibility. Their benefit to the grasslands, however, was negligible because as soon as sunlight arrived the following morning it evaporated what little moisture the ground had managed to hoard.

For Jack Padgett the rainfall was neither a curse nor a blessing. As he rode through it, he had to assume he was on the right course because the clouds had quickened, darkness had arrived, and he could no longer see tracks. He shrugged into a slicker without stopping to dismount and found an abandoned line shack to hole up in for the night. He simply accepted the rainfall. But as he took up the trail again at the grey arrival of predawn, he had his reward: the moistened earth took imprints very well.

He had indeed been on the right track. The outlaws were heading southeast, which would be the route down into New Mexico, and perhaps from there down across the south desert into Old Mexico.

He'd overtake them before that. He vaguely remembered seeing them around town before the robbery; they might be as rawhide-tough as they had looked, and he knew for a fact they were well mounted because he had seen their animals during the uproar in town. But his own big horse was less breedy and stronger, and Padgett himself had not deviated from his professional purpose and the requirements it imposed on a man in fifteen years. He had ridden down more men like these than anyone had any idea.

Daybreak was at hand when he found where they had halted to rest their animals. The boot tracks indicated that they had stood together out in the open getting rained on for perhaps as long as an hour. Behind a scrub mesquite he found a torn and soiled flour sack that was empty. He stowed it in a saddle pocket and was turning to mount up when he faintly heard riders.

There seemed to be four of them. They were coming down his back trail with carbines across their laps. Padgett's thin mouth tightened.

Vigilante townsmen. He mounted and reined ahead at an easy lope hoping to either elude them or outdistance them.

Piute Valley's southernmost rim was a series of curving upthrusts that did not deserve to be called mountains, although in places they were heavily timbered and stood at a respectable height.

The outlaws were making directly for them now. He stood in his stirrups. He was crossing open grassland in full sunshine. He could not see them even though there was at least ten miles of open country before the timber could be reached. He settled down watching the onward flow of range. They had seen him, otherwise they would not be hiding in one of the arroyos up ahead. He smiled. Fools got cautious and hid. The best outlaws he had gone after did not stop even if they knew he had them in sight; they understood perfectly what this kind of a chase amounted to. Movement; a horse race pure and simple.

Those damned clodhoppers were still following. They were miles back now, made small by distance and the empty immensity, but they were still coming, and no doubt there would be others behind this bunch.

Marshal Padgett was irritated but resigned. He'd had this occur before too. He hauled down to a slogging walk and rode on a loose rein while the sun climbed and heat arrived. The tracks were perfect; a blind man could have followed them. If those outlaws had anticipated the rainfall they probably would not have raided Juniper until it was over and the ground was hard again.

Marshal Padgett only occasionally glanced downward. Mostly, he studied the country up ahead. The difficulty with this kind of land was that it all looked flat; a man did not see a depression or an arroyo until he was almost on the verge of it, and a lot of lawmen had been shot off their horses before they had any inkling they were approaching a sunken place where armed men were waiting.

Clearly the outlaws had planned to head south down into New Mexico, and it seemed to Marshal Padgett that the one professional thing they had done was to raid the town in the afternoon so they would have oncoming darkness as their ally when they fled.

His eyes settled upon an isolated upthrust of scabrous black rocks with a few measly jack pines growing among them. He spat, kept his eye on the rocks, and smiled without a shred of humor. The dumb bastards hadn't benefited from darkness after all because it had rained.

Beyond the ugly old rocks the land dipped

then rose, and farther southward it gradually lost its appearance of flatness as it ran toward the southernmost rim of Piute Valley.

The tracks did not head directly for that gathering of broken rocks, a few of which stood plinthlike, as high as a mounted man. They went west of that place.

Marshal Padgett paralleled the rocks, watching them from beneath the shade of his tugged-forward hatbrim without turning his head in that direction. He was still following the tracks toward the somewhat broken country southward.

He wanted to see a reflection off the belt or bridle or gunbarrel of someone among those rocks, but there was no such signal.

He knew by instinct he was riding into a showdown and slightly wagged his head. If the damned fools had seen him, by now they must also have seen that little bunch of horsemen several miles back. They should have got astride and scattered like quail as they raced for the protection of the timbered slopes. He could have pursued only one of them. But men like these who remained together felt confident in their numbers.

Marshal Padgett spat cotton. The sun was climbing, it was getting hot, and he was thirsty. When the distant rocks were slightly behind him and on his left, and the tracks began to bend around in a long-spending curve eastward, he dismounted and walked ahead leading the horse. An ambushed man on a horse had no place to go; a man on foot had both mobility and tall grass.

The curving course of the tracks told him that he had been a least partly correct, they probably had not seen the rocks while heading toward the rim in the darkness before dawn, and when they had seen the townsmen it had also been light enough by then for them to see him. They had made that big swooping eastward curve and had settled into the rocks. Their horses had needed a respite, and now they had the lawman on his big strong horse closing in on them from their back trail and those quite-distant riders also approaching. It was too late to bust clear unless they wanted to be shot at by the lawman, so they would dispose of him first, then ride like the wind before that little band farther back could get close.

Padgett paused to lift his hat, mop off sweat and resettle the hat. He knew where they were and that they were watching his every move like hawks. He did not have to go after them, all he had to do was squat just beyond Winchester range and let the townsmen come up. He squinted northward where a vastly wide blaze of sunlight through rain-washed air tele-scoped distances, and for the first time he was able to count the townsmen. They were no longer riding bunched up. There were five of them, not four.

He returned his attention to the ruptured earth where those black rocks protruded like charred bones with eight or ten unthrifty scrub pine trees growing among them to provide the only protection from the heat.

Southward a blue haze was misting between Marshal Padgett and Piute Valley's southern boundary of rim rocks, and where soft breezes touched it the heat haze undulated.

He squatted to take his time studying the approaches to the rocks. The country was not as flat in this area, but there was no timber nor even any underbrush. He would have to use the eroison gullies, the breaks and arroyos to get closer.

He could have gone at them as he had done with those horsethieves. The reason he did not even consider it this time was because the horse-thieves had been watching old Macklin and he had been able to come up behind them almost within Winchester range before they had seen him. The outlaws in the rocks could not be surprised that way.

He arose, pulled down the Winchester from

its saddle-boot, and stood a moment looking in the direction of the men he could not see. Then he left the horse and walked southward to the first arroyo and disappeared down into it.

The grass was greener down here. It was also either the home or the feeding area of small animals, for although he did not see any he heard them scurrying in alarm.

The arroyo was deep enough to shield him from outside view for about thirty or forty yards, then it tilted as the result of catching silt from deluges over the centuries. When he got that far, he had to crouch.

He could not quite get into a flanking position, but that was not what he'd had in mind from the beginning. He had wanted to find their horses. Outlaws on foot were as superfluous as teats on a man.

Very carefully flattening against the north slope of the arroyo and removing his hat, Marshall Padgett used one black-gloved hand to reach slowly and very gently to part the grass as he belly-squirmed up the slanting slope. They knew he was in this arroyo, somewhere, and they would also know that if he was near the east end he would be within Winchester range. They would be as intent as rattlers on watching for movement.

He parted the grass a few stalks at a time so

as not to create movement, rested his chin in gritty soil, and with his left arm outstretched, opened a pathway through which he could see one horse dozing where it stood in shade beside the tree it was tied to.

He leaned very gently and widened the opening, looking for the other horses, but he did not see them. He brought back his arm an inch at a time, finally slid back down the slope, and turned to sit up and brush himself off. It was hotter in the arroyo than it had been above it, and the stillness was almost deafening in its silence. He was not the only one who was sweating hard.

He went back the way he had come until it was no longer necessary to crouch. Straightened up, he moved both arms and shoulders to loosen them and looked for a way over into the arroyo south of the one he was standing in. What he needed was an opening and he found it where in prehistoric times this arroyo was filled with water that had cut through at the lowest place to flood the next arroyo. He crept over into that one and turned eastward again.

This was a narrower but much deeper gulch, and it also ran in the same direction. He paused twice to listen. They knew the area he was in, and by now they would have crawling nerves. In these circumstances some men would not wait to be hunted down, they would do something — try to escape, or start out on their own desperate manhunt.

He heard nothing until a hawk circling far overhead made a shrill, incongruous chicklike squeak.

This time he had an ally in his choice of an arroyo. It not only hid him but also when he thought he was about where he had been at the limit of the other gully, this one curved around toward the rear of the rocks and continued to turn with no trace of accumulated silt.

10

Four half-started little scrub pines that had sprouted from seeds and were no more than thirty inches tall were aligned above Marshal Padgett upon the lip of his arroyo. There was almost no grass here because the ground was leached-out gravel shale.

He balanced the chances and decided they were in his favor. Raised up to his full height, he strained to achieve a little more elevation, found he still lacked six inches of being able to see out, and went searching for something to stand on. What he found was two slatey flat rocks that he placed atop one another, then he had the elevation he needed.

Placing his hat aside and using the Winchester for balance, he stepped up in a crouch and very slowly straightened up. Through the bristly little fragile limbs of the pine shoots he saw all three horses. One of them was lying down with its legs folded beneath it like a dog, even though it had its bridle and saddle on. If Jim Danforth had been there he would have said this horse had either sore feet or sore shoulders.

Marshal Padgett was as motionless as stone, eyes blocking in areas of speckled tree and rock shade. He could not locate the men among the rocks but he distinctly heard someone say, "Son of a bitch. We can't stay here forever."

His answer came in a less-troubled tone of voice. "Bust out of here now and for him it'll be like shootin' crows off a fence."

"What about them other ones? Another fifteen minutes and they'll ride up."

This time the calm voice permitted an interlude of silence to pass before replying. "There wasn't no guarantees and you knew it."

The agitated man got angry. "Guarantees your butt, Sam. We got to get down among them trees into the mountains. They're goin' to surround these rocks and. . . . What are them horses starin' at?"

Marshal Padgett eased down out of sight very slowly. Except for the horse lying down like a dog, the animals had probably detected a strange man scent because Padgett was certain they had been unable to see him. But in either case it amounted to the same thing. He stepped silently off the rocks and went briskly northward where the arroyo had a cut bank and crouched under there where it was half dark.

He waited a long time but no one appeared upon the verge looking down. If someone had he would have shot him. Gradually easing down the Winchester's hammer and shaking his shoulders to rid them of some crumbly soil, he climbed beneath the overhanging lip of earth and went quickly northward until he could see up ahead where the arroyo petered out on an uplift toward the flat ground.

He went up there until he had to crouch, then pressed close to the west bank, nearly placing a gloved hand upon a great hairy tarantula which remained motionless until it crouched to spring. He violently struck it aside.

Someone was moving, he could hear little stones rattling. A not-quite-distinct voice said, "Where *is* that bastard?" There was no answer. Moments later the same voice rose a little. "Look yonder. There's five of 'em." There still was no reply and as Marshal Padgett eased up this time, he brought the Winchester up with him.

The man was standing with the horses, evidently willing to go that far but no farther to see what had interested the animals. His Winchester was up across his body ln both hands; the man was tall, lanky, stained, soiled and unshaven, and he was standing very stiff and slightly knee-sprung, wound as tight as a steel spring with his back toward Marshal Padgett. He moved his head slowly from side to side, straining to see in the southward direction of that first arroyo where Padgett had disappeared.

Suddenly the man spat his words out. "Crap! I don't give a damn, I'm going to run for it. Look up there. Gawdammit that makes six of 'em, an' when that bunch gets down here... you can stay but I'm leaving!"

Marshal Padgett used the man's agitated noise to bring the carbine up and push it along the ground. Then he stood erect enough so that his head and shoulders were exposed as he pressed the butt-plate into his shoulder, took a long rest with his bent left hand beneath the barrel's wooden housing, and took careful aim before he cocked the weapon. As his target started at that sound and would have spun around, Marshal Padgett shot him between the shoulders. It was a perfectly performed act of execution. The outlaw had no time to cry out, but his tensed muscles reacted violently. He flung his arms out, lost his Winchester, sprang rigidly ahead, struck a tree to which a horse was tied, and ricocheted sideward falling in a threshing heap. The tied horse sat back, broke one rein but was still held fast by the other one. Gradually he came up on it, shaking and rolling his eyes.

Marshal Padgett dropped down and ran swiftly back the way he had come. He was fifty feet southward before the gunshots sounded and gouts of dirt exploded up where he had been. He hoisted one of those flat rocks he had used earlier and hurled it with all his strength in that direction. It landed with a resounding noise. Someone above him and to his right fired again as he was hoisting himself atop the remaining flat stone, carbine swinging ahead. He was exposed again as he yanked the gun into his shoulder, searching for a target. There was greasy grey black-powder smoke among the rocks, which added to the hindrance of visibility, but he caught movement where someone was levering up for another shot. He waited for the outlaw to lean out of his concealment, either to fire again or to look over where he had been aiming.

The man moved in jerks, gripping his Winchester too far back to be able to raise it and reposition his hands, even if he had seen Marshal Padgett. But he did not see him — his lean, weather-bronzed face was pointing in the direction he had been shooting. Marshal Padgett

116

had his head, shoulders, both arms and part of his upper body in sight as he aimed, held his breath for a second, and squeezed the trigger.

The outlaw's whole body came up off the ground between two rough dark rocks as though propelled from behind. The bullet had penetrated him through the upper left arm, through the chest, and exited as flat as a mushroom in the armpit of his right arm. The man did not die as quickly as Marshal Padgett's first victim. He plunged forward, struggled up onto all fours and hung there like a gutshot bear with blood pouring from his mouth. He finally eased over slowly to one side and came to rest very gently against the ground.

Marshal Padgett dropped down and went swiftly back around the curve of the arroyo to stop and listen. There was not a sound. Even the reverberations he had detected earlier of those oncoming townsmen had ceased.

Sweat had darkened both the front and back of his shirt. It ran across his forehead to gather between his eyes and run down his nose where it dripped off. He ignored it and twisted to scan the nearly perpendicular bank of the arroyo for another place to achieve sufficient elevation to be able to see out.

There was no such advantage. He shook off the sweat and continued back around the way he had come. There were places back there, but he would then be facing the rocks, which was something he had chosen not to do earlier. Now he had flanked them, had killed two, and the third one would be rigid with fear, unable to guess where the killer might appear next.

The silence was depthless and it drew out endlessly. Marshal Padgett came to one of the places he could raise up enough to see beyond. There was grass, pale and over two feet tall, with seedheads forming. He pushed a gloved hand into it and crouched back waiting, but no gunshot erupted. He moved a couple of yards to his left and this time as he raised up to part the grass, he did it so carefully that the stalks only very minutely swayed.

He could see the rocks very well. He could see only one horse but he could see fading gunsmoke. He shifted slightly to look farther up-country, around in front of the rocks. The reason he had not heard moving horses up there was because those five riders from Juniper were sitting well beyond Winchester range, as still and motionless as statues. He shifted back toward the rocks.

A man called in a croaking voice. "I quit. . . I'll fling my guns out. . . . Y'hear me out there? I give up. Here come the guns."

Padgett saw the six-gun sail toward his arroyo

but five yards to his right. It was followed by the Winchester. The man called again. "Awright? Hey, *say something*! I know you're down in there somewhere."

Marshall Padgett flicked off more sweat and neither moved nor spoke.

Now the outlaw tasted real fear. He had disarmed himself and there had been no answer to his offer to surrender. He called again, in a hoarser voice this time.

"Listen, mister...the money's all here. You killed the other two. I tossed out my guns. For Chris'sake what more do you want?"

Marshal Padgett began to straighten up slowly, raising the Winchester as he finally called out. "Walk out of the rocks!"

The outlaw may have discerned something in the cold, flat voice, or he may have finally succumbed to the deep horror that had gripped him since he had witnessed those two killings. Whatever it was he remained in hiding and did not call out again.

Marshal Padgett raised up until he could see about where the man was, gauged the distance, balanced his chances of utilizing the rocks as the outlaws had done — by keeping them in front of his body — and tested the footing. Once he was beyond the arroyo he could move too fast for anyone to hold him in their sights for more than a second. It was while he was struggling up out of the arroyo that he would be most vulnerable.

He believed what he had told Doc Winthrop at the Juniper jailhouse office one time: There were no guarantees. He tested the ground; it was slightly spongy from light rainfall. He watched the rocks, speculating that his adversary might be searching for the weapons the dead men had dropped. He took down a couple of deep breaths, slammed the Winchester butt down hard and, using it to vault with, rose up awkwardly over the lip of the arroyo. Feeling the bank crumbling beneath him as he wrenched the carbine upward, he rolled frantically for five feet, then leapt up and ran directly toward the rocks. Nothing happened that he was aware of, but northward where those stiffly erect horsemen were sitting, there was a little flurry as they saw Marshal Padgett come rising up out of the ground and run toward the rocks.

He could not avoid making noise. From behind the rocks there was more noise as a frightened man scrambled desperately in the direction of his two dead companions; it seemed he was finally convinced that there was not going to be any surrender.

Marshal Padgett slammed into one of the foremost tall rocks. Its pointed head rose three feet above him. He leaned the carbine aside, palmed his ivory-stocked Colt, cocked it, and pushed it around into a wide slit between his rock and the one adjoining it. No one fired so he eased his twisting body around until he could see among the trees and the other rocks.

The outlaw was on his knees beside the first man Padgett had shot near the horses — all three of which were quaking but unmoving. He had found the carbine and had it in his hand when he looked back, saw the cocked Colt and the man behind it. He dropped the Winchester and threw up both arms as he cried out. "I quit."

Without haste Marshal Padgett squeezed between the rocks and stopped when the kneeling man was twenty feet in front. He raised the Colt slowly. The outlaw saw it coming and sprang erect, color draining beneath his bronzed features. He yelled. *"I quit!"*

Marshal Padgett squeezed the trigger. There was a ten-second echo. The horse that had already broken one rein threw his weight backward again and this time the remaining rein broke. He whirled and fled. It had not been so much the gunblast that had terrified him, but the hurtling body of the outlaw striking him in the chest and left shoulder.

The man seemed to be struggling to turn over onto his stomach as Marshal Padgett holstered the Colt and went over where the other two horses had been unable to break free. He calmed them with quiet words so that he could remove a canteen suspended from a saddlehorn and tip his head as he drank deeply. He had been thirsty since he had first arrived down here and nothing had happened over the past couple of hours to alleviate that.

He replaced the canteen, patted the horse on the neck, then walked over northward to the last fringes of shade and watched two of those townsmen riding in a flinging race to try and overtake the fleeing outlaw horse.

He saw them finally catch it and start back. Shortly now they would ride down here. Marshal Padgett went back and emptied the pockets of the dead men, tossing aside such things as pocket watches and clasp knives. All the letters and money he found he carefully folded and placed into his own pockets. Then he stepped over the last man he had shot, who was no longer moving, and got another drink from the canteen. This time the horse did not even flinch. The man had talked softly to him and had patted him. The horse knew a person to be trusted when he saw one.

Finally Marshal Padgett walked back out into the blazing afternoon sunlight, ignoring the oncoming townsmen heading for his own animal. He patted it too before swinging up and reining at a slow walk back in the direction of the rocks. There were now five more horses without riders standing appreciatively in shade while their awed and silent owners walked behind the rocks and stopped dead still.

The sun was about to begin its long final swing toward the very distant haze-obscured westerly peaks. It had baked Piute Valley since rising this morning; all the meager benefits of that light rain last night had long been negated.

A second group of riders, four of them, were loping toward the rocks. Marshal Padgett stopped to study these newcomers. They were too distant to be recognized but he knew rangemen when he saw them.

He continued to ride slowly toward the rocks.

11

He recognized the townsmen from having seen them in Juniper. Except for one man — a sinewy redhead called Will who had been Don Myser's swamper at the blacksmith shop — he did not know their names.

He nodded to them as he walked back where they were standing in gun-smoke-scented shade, got the canteen for another drink, and offered it around. No one accepted. He looped it back around the saddlehorn and tugged at his gloves as he said, "They made a fight of it."

The five men from Juniper neither looked up nor spoke. Marshal Padgett had encountered this before: shock, loss of color, loss of speech. They worked around town, probably had never seen dead men before. He broke the silence. "Thanks for catching the loose horse. If you gents will lend me a hand we'll get 'em tied over their saddles and head back."

Two of the pale men twisted at the same time. One of them said, "Someone is coming."

Burt Standish came in among the trees before halting to dismount. His three hired men did the same, and when they got closer and saw the dead men they stopped and gazed at Marshal Padgett. He knew Burt, at least by sight. He nodded toward him. "I got the money back. I'll need a little help."

Unlike the white-faced townsmen Standish and his riders got untracked. One of them cut the broken reins up close to the bit and looped a lariat around this horse so he could be led from the saddle. His companions worked methodically loading the corpses and only glanced around curiously when the townsmen walked away. Burt said, "What's wrong with them, Marshal?"

Padgett shrugged. "The sight of blood."

Burt accepted that and made a final lash. "I'd say it was quite a fight," he said.

Padgett answered matter-of-factly. "Yes it was, and it got hot down in the arroyo where I had to go to get behind them."

One of the Patterson-ranch cowboys looked with awe at the marshal. He had been up yonder with the others and had seen Jack Padgett fight it out with those horsethieves. He had a world of respect for Marshal Padgett.

When the law officer left them to go out where his big horse was patiently waiting, this awed cowboy looked over his shoulder before saying, "This one I been lashin' to the saddle — he was hit square between the shoulders from behind."

Standish, who had noticed this earlier, and who had seen a horsethief with the same kind of fatal wound a month or so back, spoke without raising his head. "It can happen in a ruckus. Let's gather their weapons and get out of here." Burt led one horse with his riders bringing the other animals.

Out where the townsmen were clustered in sunlight, heads turned to watch the stockmen appear. Marshal Padgett rode around there and offered to take one lead rope, but Burt's men swung up holding the shanks. They did not need help.

Burt turned northward beside Marshal Padgett. They made a careless wide slant in the direction of town with the townsmen trailing close behind the rangemen and the lead horses.

For a long time there was nothing said back among the rangemen and townsmen. Up ahead where the marshal and the rangeboss were riding, when Burt wanted to hear the details Marshal Padgett obliged him.

There were a couple of things left out, otherwise the recitation was true to the facts. Burt watched his horse's ears and slouched in silence for a while before building a smoke, lighting it, and twisting to glance back. Everything was in order so he sat forward and said, "Did you know Arley Patton, Marshal?"

Padgett nodded. He was squinting toward the lowering sun in order to make an estimate of how long it would be before they reached town.

"Well, he's dead."

Marshal Padgett turned his head. Arley had been standing near him in front of the saloon.

"Did you know Myser the blacksmith? He's dead too. And that 'breed-looking feller who run the cafe."

Jack Padgett watched Burt inhale and exhale. Myser, too, had been within arm's reach back in front of the saloon. "Anyone else?" he asked, and Burt brushed ash off his shirt before replying.

"Yeah. Jeremiah Macklin — and that old man who worked for Mister Nevins in the general store." Burt met the lawman's gaze. "And that snifflin' feller who worked for Jim Danforth as his dayman."

Marshal Padgett waited and when Burt offered no more names Padgett squared around in silence and looked up ahead. "That was a massacre," he finally stated. Burt agreed by nodding his head as he stumped out the quirley atop his saddlehorn.

"I don't give a damn how you done it, Marshal, I'm just real glad that you did."

Padgett neither glanced at the rangeboss nor spoke a word.

Burt had another sentence to add. "I just wish to hell I could have been there too."

They made fair time considering the difficulty in keeping three slack burdens from flopping off-balance when the horses loped. The townsmen remained back with the lead stock and did not approach Marshal Padgett even at a rest-halt just after dusk when the horses were watered at a creek and the men sprung their legs, checked the lashings and knots, and stood idly smoking and conversing.

In fact by the time they came up into Juniper from the south, with darkness blanketing everything, the townsmen were still avoiding the town marshal.

Jim Danforth heard them approaching, rubbed his eyes, and heaved up out of the harness-room chair to walk out front. As the cavalcade turned in, Jim's wooden expression did not alter when he went ahead to help lift the corpses down. His dumbshock had eventually ended sometime the previous night. Today, he had gone about his chores with a sense of outrage. Now, as the others took horses inside to be cared for, Jim stood above the laid-out corpses. These were the men who had killed some of Jim's friends of long-standing, such as Arley and Don Myser, old Angus up at the store. He wanted to curse them, to lay his hands on them.

Marshal Padgett strolled up and said, "I'd take it kindly if you'd have someone take them up to Doc's shed in the morning."

Danforth bitterly assented. "Yeah. . . . I wish just one of them was still alive." Jim raised large thick hands. "I'd strangle him an' make it take a half hour for him to die."

Marshal Padgett walked northward carrying a booted Winchester hooked in the bend of one arm. Around him Juniper was mostly dark and silent. At the jailhouse he lighted his lamp and stoked up the stove. It was very late and it was also cold. It had been a long time since he had eaten and it would be another four or five hours before the cafe would be open in the morning. If it opened.

He set a bottle of whisky atop the desk, got out the cleaning rod, swabs and oil, and sat down to unload the carbine before giving it a thorough cleaning.

He took one drink from the bottle and left it standing.

After racking the Winchester and turning down the stove damper, he blew out the lamp, then locked the jailhouse from the outside and went up to his room. It was dark as pitch in the hallway; when he entered his room he ignored the little lamp and bedded down. The last thing he heard was a group of horsemen heading up out of town past the rooming house and drowsily thought it would be the men from Patterson ranch.

The night was utterly still and cold, a good night for sleeping. Marshal Padgett did not open his eyes until the sun was climbing. He was a little sore in the muscles and joints, but most of all he was starved.

Outside it was a beautiful morning to walk in. He went down to the cafe and, because it was more than an hour later than most of the customers of the cafe ate breakfast, there was only one diner when he walked in. The thick, dark-looking woman who came woodenly to take his order flicked her eyes over him and said, "I hope it took 'em a long time to die, Marshal. They killed my husband."

Jack Padgett watched her walk away.

By the time he got over to the jailhouse he had noticed the silence, the lack of people on

130

the plankwalks, and the planking which had been nailed over the door of Nevins's store.

He fired up the stove to chase away the lingering chill and carefully emptied his pockets. Sitting forward he sifted through the personal effects of the men he had killed and wrote down three names on a piece of paper. Then he swept everything into a desk drawer and made a fresh pot of coffee before returning to the desk with a box of wanted posters.

He was midway through and had located fugitive posters on two of the dead men when Walt Nevins walked in. The marshal looked up and nodded. "You were lucky from what I hear, Mister Nevins. Have a cup of java, I just made it."

Nevins sat down instead. Last night when he had told his daughter that the marshal had gone after those killers, she had walked out of the parlor leaving him looking after her.

But whatever had happened between Bessie and the marshal had been pushed far back in Nevins's mind. Padgett eyed him and leaned to push something to the edge of the desk. "That's the money I took off them. I didn't count it but they didn't get a chance to spend it so it all ought to be there."

Walt eyed the crumpled notes. "I don't see how it could have happened like that," he finally said. "Just all at once." He raised stricken eyes to Jack Padgett's handsome, tanned and composed face. "In five minutes they killed half the businessmen in Juniper. Without any warning, just commenced killing people, perfect strangers. They'd been in my store not three hours earlier buying smokin' tobacco. It set the town back fifteen years, Marshal." He glanced at the money again. "Good God I would have given it to them. I'd have handed it over in a minute. Marshal, why didn't they just walk in and point their guns at me? They could have had the money and anythin' else in the store. They didn't have to dynamite the safe and kill old Angus, then try to kill everyone else in sight."

Marshal Padgett leaned back in the chair eyeing Nevins. Women stayed shocked; men usually didn't. He sighed and refilled his cup over at the stove, then walked back to the desk and sat down, looking impatiently at the box of dodgers. He still had to find the poster on that third one.

Nevins finally arose. "I'm glad you caught them," he said in a tone of voice that was finally beginning to lose its edge of stunned incomprehension. "I hope they were lookin' straight into your gun barrel when you killed them." He walked out of the office and Marshal Padgett went back to sifting through the box of dodgers.

He found it. The third man was named Alex Bowie and he was wanted in Idaho for murder and robbery. The bounty was five hundred dollars. Marshal Padgett wrote the name on his slip of paper with the other names on it, then shook his head. Idaho must not consider murderers worth much.

He put the box on the floor behind the desk and drew several sheets of writing paper from a drawer. Outside, the town was still very quiet. He heard a rider in the roadway northward. Over at the smithy where someone was usually working steel over the anvil this time of day, the place was locked up and empty.

Juniper was like a graveyard until shortly after noon when four men with digging tools went up through town in one of Danforth's least valuable old wagons heading in the direction of Cemetery Hill. Marshal Padgett watched them pass through one of the little barred front-wall windows and thought that it would probably be the biggest funeral Juniper had ever had. He was right, it would be.

He lit a cheroot and leaned back, totaling up the money due him. It came to a respectable figure. His gaze fell upon the soiled, crumpled greenbacks Nevins had neglected to take with him, and he put them into a desk drawer.

The stove was cooling which was just as well because midday heat was beginning to come through the roof and walls of the jailhouse.

He had put on a clean shirt and britches this morning but his hat was soiled so he spent a little time vigorously brushing it before leaving the jailhouse to make a leisurely round of the town. The air was clear and soft-scented, there was not a cloud in sight. It was a magnificent summer day. There was a saddle horse dozing at the tie-rack out front of Doctor Winthrop's place. Some cowboy had probably hurt his back getting bucked off.

12

Doc had not slept well. At midnight he had arisen to go to the kitchen for some watered whisky. After that he was able to sleep until someone's dog across the back alley began barking excitedly in front of a squirrel hole.

He went out back with Swen to place corpses into coffins and left it up to Swen how the boxes would be taken out to Cemetery Hill later in the day. Afterward he returned to the house and sat down in his cluttered, dusty little office, dug through the accumulation of debris in a desk drawer until he found what he was searching for, then drew it forth, carefully peeled off the tinfoil and struck a match to light the cigar. It was as dry as toast and Doc had not smoked in several years, but aside from a fit of coughing he grimly persevered, filling the little room with bluish smoke.

He did not hear the horseman ride up out front and until there was a rattling loud noise at the front door Doc had no idea he had a visitor.

He left the cigar to die a belated death in the office and walked out front. The face of the bronzed, husky man standing on the porch made Doc's heart miss a beat, but he recovered quickly and led the rangeman back to the office. He had to open a window for the cigar smoke to depart. It was stuck tight from long disuse, and Doc cursed and strained until it opened.

He watched the husky rangeman remove his hat carefully and balance it upon one knee where he sat. He knew Mitchell Smith simply from having seen him many times through the years, and they had talked a few times, but that was the extent of it. Well, not quite the extent of it; Doc knew something about this quiet, capable-looking rangeman that had shocked him when he had heard it, something which no one else knew now that Jeremiah was dead. The burden was left with Doc and he damned well didn't like it.

He said, "I expect you came because you heard that Mister Macklin is dead."

The cowboy nodded, light brown eyes solemn.

Doc fidgeted; he had never liked these strong silent types. He liked a man who would let his emotions show.

"Well, it was the day before yesterday when three strangers raided the town."

Smith said, "I've heard all that, Doctor."

Doc shifted on his chair. "Yes. Well, Jeremiah was out at the front gate with me, and when he saw them with guns he yelled something which I could not make out and started running toward them...hobbling toward them, his leg was giving him hell. He got down almost as far as Sam Starr's shop when one of those fellers turned in the saddle and shot Jeremiah — they killed several people. I got down where Jeremiah was lying. He was conscious and losing blood fast. I poured laudanum down him to stop the pain. Jim Danforth helped me carry him up here."

"Where was he shot, Doctor?"

"A tad to the left of his breastbone. Otherwise he'd have died where he fell. Mister Smith, if I'd cut him open to try and stop the internal bleeding he'd have died anyway. Jeremiah was old. He was tough, I'll grant you, but he hasn't been fit for a couple of years now. Only I never had the nerve to tell him that."

"I know," Mitchell Smith said quietly.

"Well, we were friends for a long time. I didn't want to cut him open, put him through that. So I took some watered whisky in and we drank it, and he smiled. I swear I hadn't seen him smile five times in twenty years. He smiled, lay back with his eyes closed, and died."

Doc rose to pace to the open window. "Do you know Swen Jorgenson the carpenter around town?"

"No."

"Well, a little while before you came along I helped Swen close the coffins. The others we'll bury this afternoon. I set Jeremiah on sawhorses near the back of the shed because I figured someone from the ranch would be along to take him home to be buried."

Mitchell Smith rose and dropped on his hat. "I'll send in a wagon, Doctor. What about the men who killed him?"

Doc faced around. "They're in there too. Marshal Padgett went after them, caught them a long way south of town and killed them."

"How many?"

"Three," replied Doc and saw the look on the younger man's face.

Smith said, "He's handy, Doctor." Then he displayed a little sad smile and changed the subject. "It'll take a lot of getting used to. I been on the ranch since I was pretty young. I guess if I was to stay there now, which I likely won't because the place'll get sold, I'd never get used to not seeing Jeremiah come stumping across the yard. . . . I didn't aim to take up so much of your time."

Doc watched the husky man walk out of the office and almost threw up a hand to stop him. Instead, he trooped after him as far as the porch before reaching a decision. Out there he said, "You'll be coming back with the wagon?"

Mitchell Smith nodded and walked out to his horse. Doc lingered in the doorway. He had perhaps until late this evening to figure out what he should do — if he should do anything. As he closed the door he could almost feel old Jeremiah standing in the shadows looking at him. He glared. "Damn you anyway; why didn't you just take your confounded secret with you! What'd you lay it on me for?"

He was returning to the office when someone knocked and he had to turn and go back. This time the caller was no older than Mitchell Smith had been, but he was slight and sinewy and had a shock of red hair. Doc irritably motioned for the young man to enter and closed the door with unnecessary noise as he said, "Unless you are real sick I'm awful busy today. . . . You worked for Don Myser didn't you?"

The red-haired man said, "Yes. I've helped with your rig and buggy horse a lot of times. My name is Will Logan an' I ain't sick."

Doc considered the young man's drawn face and gestured toward one of the chairs in his parlor-waiting room. Logan sat down, clasped both hands between his knees, and watched Doctor Winthrop take another chair. He continued to stare without saying a word until Doc scowled at him.

"All right, Mister Logan, if you're not sick, then what brought you up here? Like I said, I'm busy today."

The silence ran on a little longer before Logan spoke. "I want to tell someone something. You got them fellers in your embalmin' shed that Marshal Padgett killed yestiddy?"

"Yes, I have them out there."

"Well, me and four other fellers from town went after the marshal to help if he run them men to earth."

Doc fidgeted, his face beginning to get red.

Will Logan seemed not to notice. "He was already after them when we come down there. He was in a ditch commencing to stalk them. Us fellers stopped out a ways when there was a gunshot. We didn't want to ride into gun range. . . . It took a while, Doctor — there was a lot of shootin' for a spell. Then it slacked off, and after a bit there was one shot. We couldn't see no one. They was hiding among some big black old rocks shaded by a few runty pine trees. We couldn't see him after that but we heard a man yell out 'I quit' as clear as you an' me talkin' in this room. He yelled it like he was scairt to death. After that we saw Marshal Padgett jump out of a ditch and run to the rocks. Then there was one more shot. That was the last one. Directly the marshal come out and went back where his horse was, and us fellers finally rode down there in among the rocks. There was a feller lying there shot at close range right between the eyes. The other two was also dead. One shot through the back, another one shot from the left side through to the right side. But the feller shot between the eyes, he was still tricklin' blood when we got over there. . . . He didn't have a gun. . . . There was a Winchester lyin' near the feller who got back-shot, but the feller he shot in the fore-head didn't have no weapon at all."

Doc's color drained, leaving his face grey. He did not take his eyes off the blacksmith's helper for a long time. Then he made an effort to rally as he quietly said, "Son, why did you come up here and tell me this?"

Logan made a little fluttery gesture with his hands. "Mister Myser set a lot of store by you. He used to say if Piute Valley had a conscience, you was it. . . . Well, I never was sure what that meant but he set a lot of store by you, and I was

141

awake all last night...I never saw anythin' like that before....I just wanted to get it out, is all, and with Mister Myser gone..."

Doc arose. "How old are you?"

The sinewy man also stood up. "Twenty-one."

Doc led the way to the kitchen where he half-filled two cups with watered whisky and handed one cup to Will Logan. "You are old enough to drink that, so you're old enough to make sense out of what I'm going to tell you." Doc paused to half drain his cup, and with color returning to his face he looked fiercely at the younger man. "Don't you ever tell another soul what you just told me, as long as you're in this valley. Maybe someday it will be all right for you to say it again, but you listen to me. You just called Marshal Padgett a murderer. Do you know what he'd do if he heard that you'd said that of him?"

Will Logan sipped from the cup with his eyes fixed on Doc's face. When he lowered the cup he nodded his head. "Yes sir, I got an idea about what he'd do. Only I'm not the only one who knows what he did. There was four other fellers with me."

Doc finished his watered whisky and put the cup aside. "Did you talk about it on the ride back?"

"Yes. We all did. And we stayed clear of the

marshal, and two of 'em was in the cafe this morning when I was havin' breakfast and they started talkin' about it all over again." Young Logan put his cup aside with its contents scarcely touched. "I'll do like you say, but there was five fellers seen that, Doctor, an' later when them rangemen come up — Mister Standish of Patterson ranch — they seen those dead men too. I'd say a man wouldn't have to be awful smart to know what happened. Doctor, there was four of them countin' Mister Standish and five of us, an' we all know what happened among them rocks. . . . I won't say a word, but that's just one feller out of nine."

Doc leaned on the kitchen table. He felt like a drowning man. Gun-downed men were swamping him. In one day he'd cleaned up six corpses of men he'd known since arriving in Piute Valley. Then there were the three outlaws still in the shed to be cared for. Before that there was a cowboy named Cal Vincent who'd been so drunk when he'd died he could barely stand. And four horsethieves. And two others.

Doc and death were old acquaintances but not like this. He put a hand upon the young man's shoulder and walked him back to the waiting room. As he reached for the door latch he said, "Well, at least you keep out of it. I understood what you were gettin' at in the kitchen: It's not going to be a secret for long. But you keep your mouth shut and stay out of it. I'll tell you something, boy, Marshal Padgett will kill you on sight if he ever hears what you've told me about him. I know that kind of a man so you can believe what I'm telling you. . . . Don't even talk about it with the men who were down there with you. Not with anyone. Not even with me again."

He let the boy out, closed the door, and returned to the kitchen looking for the cup the blacksmith's helper had barely touched. Later he heated water and shaved, something which he'd been unable to do lately. Then he went out back and across the alley, entered his shed, and barred the door from the inside, which made the windowless little building dark. He lighted a lamp and carried it with him as he leaned over each dead outlaw to make a close inspection. The man who had been killed by a bullet between the eyes he examined longest. To verify something one lamp would not help him with, he lighted a second lamp. The combined glow of both lamps showed him faint and scattered powderburns. This one had been shot in the face at close range.

When Marshal Padgett had killed this man he had done it from little more than arm's length away.

Doc blew out his lamps, locked the shed from the outside, picked up his hat on the way through the house and emerged into the afternoon brilliance just in time to be buttonholed by Sam Starr the harness maker. Sam was attired from head to foot in black, one pocket sagged from the weight of a Bible, and his gaunt face was very solemn as he said, "We sent word out that the burials will be this evening. Doc, they dug enough holes out there — but — they didn't dig none for those outlaws."

Doc nodded about that. "Bury them later, Sam. It'll be bad enough with cryin' women and bawling kids. That'd be turning a knife in the wound."

Sam's solemn expression vanished. "Exactly what I been sayin' but someone thought you might want to get those other three out of your shed today too."

That annoyed Doc. "What some damned fool says about what I'll do is poppycock. Have you seen Jim Danforth?"

Starr had. "Yes. He's down yonder dustin' off his hearse and layin' out the black harness and all." Sam cocked his head a little. "Someday Juniper might get a preacher. I tell you straight out, Doc. Every time I do this, reading from the Book and all, I get a real bad feelin' in the chest....I haven't been exactly a saint you know."

Doc considered the gaunt, rugged, hard old face and gave Starr a light, rough pat on the shoulder. "None of us have, Sam. At least you can read and you do it right well....I'll be out there."

Doc resumed his interrupted walk toward the lower end of town. His body tightened slightly as he strode past the jailhouse. The door was open so he looked in. He was thankful the office was empty. Right now Doctor Winthrop was not up to a conversation with Marshal Padgett.

They would not have met anyway. Doc was walking south and Marshal Padgett was northward, leaning on the public corrals where he had accidentally intercepted Bessie Nevins. She had a net shopping bag on her arm and freshly brushed hair that caught and softly imprisoned the slanting sunrays.

Her eyes were both troubled and quizzical as she listened to the handsome law officer.

"It'll take time, but folks will get over it. Your paw was lucky not to be in the store. I'll do my share to help folks get through it." He showed her his soft, handsome smile. "I'd like it if we could go buggy-riding again, Bessie. There's a moon tonight." His eyes held hers

146

over a long interval while she struggled with emotions he had left in shreds the last time.

"Folks think about themselves, I guess, and that's likely the way it should be, Bessie, but mostly they got families and all. It was hard on me too." He did not say he had no family, no one to turn to, nor did he have to say anything like that because she was nodding up at him, color in her cheeks for the first time in several days, brightness back in her gentle eyes.

"Would you like it if I made up a hamper; better than last time, Marshal?"

"I sure would like that, Bessie. The cafeman's wife can't cook worth a darn. I could come by for you about seven."

She smiled red and brushed his arm with light fingers, then hurried up as far as the corner and turned southward. Her father had the store open for business again. It still smelled of burnt powder and much of the damaged merchandise had not been returned to the shelves, but Walt and two hired clean-up ladies had spent more time sandstoning the dark stains on the floor than they had spent reordering the shelves.

The marshal was right, the town would recover and one indisputable sign of this was that Nevins's general store was back in business again. Like other general stores in small towns, Walt's place was more than just a store. It was also the place where people met, where social plans were made, where the community coalesced, where gossip was exchanged in whispers and also where a lot of it originated.

13

People began arriving in town from several directions long before the burial services were to take place; cowmen and their riders, wearing clean clothes and freshly brushed hats, were long-faced and not very talkative. Of the six dead men at least one of them, and in most cases all of them, had touched the lives of these range people many times. Nor was it an ordinary matter, there were five pine boxes on sawhorses out at Cemetery Hill. As one of the men from Patterson ranch told Burt Standish, it was like attending the funeral after a massacre, there were just too many of them out there waiting to be covered with dirt.

Ranch wives and townswomen in black had set up tables of food in the saloon. It was likely to be a long service and folks got hungry. They had secured permission to do this from the town council, because as far as anyone knew Arley'd had no family.

No drinks were sold. There was no one on hand to man Arley's bar, but a couple of stockmen had bottles hidden discreetly beneath buggy seats, and that helped pass the time and loosen people up who had not worn a black coat nor a necktie since the last funeral.

Jim Danforth, who had talked with Doc while vigorously shining the dead-black, elegantly carved sides of his two-horse hearse, stood back examining his work after Doc departed. Jim was satisfied although one of the angels on the off-side had half a foot missing where some idiot had bumped into the rig a couple of years back.

Jim ducked into his harness room, took two swallows from a bottle he kept hidden under a pile of sweat-stiff old saddle blankets, then returned to the run to bring in the black horses. He was not happy; aside from a steady stream of folks bringing saddle animals and rigs down to be cared for until after the buryings, it was going to be embarrassing and awkward because his hearse only hauled one coffin at a time. He was going to have to go back and forth five times and sure as hell that was going to make folks fidget while they waited for Sam Starr to commence the services.

150

He paused out back on his way to fetch in the black team and frowned at the three dozing horses that had belonged to those dead outlaws. When Doc had walked in Jim had thought he might be interested in acquiring one of those animals when the marshal auctioned them off to cover the costs for burying their former owners, but it turned out that Doc's questions had to do with the men instead. All Danforth could tell him was what he had personally seen late the night that Marshal Padgett and the others had returned from the shootout.

Doc had walked away not looking exactly happy, but Jim was not going to make up something just to please Doc or anyone else for that matter. He continued on past to get the black horses.

As a matter of fact Doctor Winthrop had not been unhappy. All he'd wanted to know was the names of all the men who had come to town behind the marshal, and Jim had given him that information with casual indifference. He'd also been interested in all that Danforth could recall of the dead men. Now, as he strode northward lost in throught, he nearly collided with Marshal Padgett just north of the jailhouse.

Padgett made an excuse for Doc. "All the work that got dumped on you lately, it's a wonder you even have time to be out here."

151

Doc looked at the handsome peace officer. "Nine," he replied, "counting the outlaws. I've been through epidemics that didn't carry off that many people."

Marshal Padgett looked thoughtful. "That many?"

Doc used his fingers to tick off names. "Myser, Patton, Macklin, old Angus, the cafeman, Jim Danforth's hostler, and the three outlaws."

Marshal Padgett looked past Doc, then over in the direction of Nevins's store, and finally back to Doc. "I got some letters to send off. I'll see you out yonder." Padgett strolled past.

Doc turned briefly to watch the tall, handsome figure, then headed for home to wash and change into his black suit.

Mitchell Smith was out in front of the house talking to one of the Macklin riders who had driven the wagon into town with him. Doc saw them before they saw him and felt more harassed than ever. When he got up to them, he nodded and beckoned for them to follow him over to the embalming shed. He should have suggested that they drive the wagon down the alley to the shed, but it did not occur to him until he was helping them pack Jeremiah's box. Jeremiah had not looked as heavy as he evidently had been.

After they had slid the box into the wagon,

Mitch Smith left it up to his companion to hoist the tailgate and run the chains across the coffin to hold it in place. Mitch leaned against a sideboard regarding Doctor Winthrop. He did not show much expression and that made Doc uncomfortable; he still did not know what he was going to do about this man.

Mitch said, "While we were waitin' for you a while back one of the fellers from over east of town come up and told us something."

Doc nodded and waited for the rest of it.

"He said there's talk around town that Marshal Padgett backshot one of those outlaws, and killed another one at close range with a bullet between the eyes."

Doc shrugged. "They are the men who killed Jeremiah, Mitchell."

Smith still showed no emotion. "Yeah. I'd probably have done the same if I'd come onto them."

"Well, I got to get dressed and—"

"Doc, I saw him do the same thing when Jeremiah and the rest of us rode after those horsethieves. One in the back when he was tryin' to run away, and another one in the face when he had his hands raised."

Doc considered Mitch Smith. If he had heard the story about the last three of Marshal Padgett's victims, then it was spreading. Not only through town but out over the range as well. What Doc – and earlier old Jeremiah – had tried very hard to prevent, was out of control; it would be a matter of time before Marshal Padgett heard it. He said, "Mitchell...there isn't anything I can say."

Smith pulled an old worn pair of gloves from a hip pocket and began putting them on as he spoke again. "Just one thing, Doctor. Is that who you got under those old blankets in the shed?"

"Yes."

The younger man's eyes came up. "It's not that I don't believe that feller who told us the story about how those men died, but as near as I can see you're the only one around who can tell me straight out: Was one of them shot in the back and other one shot in the face?"

Doc thought about temporizing, but the steady look he was getting warned him that it would not work. Quiet though Mitchell Smith was, he was a long way from being a fool. Doc said, "Yes...Mitchell, like I already said, those are the men who killed Jeremiah."

Smith's companion was climbing to the wagon seat and Mitchell also turned to climb up there. But first he said, "Yeah. And like I said, I'd most likely have killed them too if I'd got the chance, but not like that and neither would you." He settled beside his companion and looked down. "And neither would Jeremiah." The wagon started to move. It went ahead a few yards hugging the westside plankwalk, then the driver made a tight turn that nearly cramped his off-side front wheel, and walked his hitch northward out of town.

Doc had his hand on the gate as he watched the wagon. He wagged his head a little. No, maybe old Jeremiah would not have shot those men the way Padgett had, but if he had caught them with his horses he sure as hell would have hanged them. Doc started toward the house.

There was a difference, but it was a very damned fine line.

He went inside, scrubbed and changed his clothes, got into the black suit and went out to the kitchen for something to eat. This was going to be one hell of a long, distressing afternoon and evening. He hesitated for a moment, eyeing a pony-bottle of apple brandy on a shelf. He did not like brandy but the pony-bottle would fit inconspicuously in a pocket and a larger bottle of whisky would not.

He took down the bottle, pocketed it, scooped up his hat on the way out, and saw a large bearded man mantled with dust dismounting outside his gate at the tie-rack. Doc had never seen the man before but he clearly was not a rangeman. He wore a flat-crowned, stiff-brimmed dark grey hat, a baggy suit coat with britches to match and his brown boots with their flat, drover's heels matched the rest of him. He looked brown even where whiskers did not conceal his face.

Annoyance made Doc unsmiling as he walked down to the gate. It was a long mile out to Cemetery Hill. He had decided to walk rather than ask Jim to rig up his top-buggy, and it was hot. He would have walked past but the heavy-built man stopped him. He had a surprisingly mild voice for such a formidable-looking individual. He said, "Excuse me. Are you Doctor Winthrop?"

Doc nodded.

"My name is Ash Hollister. I'm a stranger hereabouts and a mile or so northward I came onto a couple of fellers in a wagon hauling a coffin. They gave me directions to your place. Doctor, I need a little information." As he said this the massively powerful man reached into a pocket and brought forth a small badge which looked even smaller on the palm of his ham-sized hand. "I'm lookin' for your town marshal, Mister Padgett."

Doc eyed the badge. Ash Hollister was the sheriff of a county up in Wyoming. He raised

156

his head wondering irritably why Mitchell Smith had directed Sheriff Hollister to him instead of on down the road to the jailhouse. He knew the answer to that without even deliberating.

Doc sighed. "Sheriff, we've had damned near a massacre in Juniper and I was on my way out to the cemetery for the services. Marshal Padgett will be out there if you're in a hurry, but I don't think it'd be the right place to walk up and introduce yourself to him."

Hollister pocketed his little badge and studied Doc's face — its dark blue, troubled eyes, its lines and general look of harassment. He spoke again in that mild tone of voice. "I expect you're right. Can you direct me to the jailhouse? I'll put up my horse, get something to eat, and wait for Mister Padgett down there."

Doc jerked his head. "Down the road. You'll see it on the west side nearly opposite the general store."

Hollister nodded and asked a question. "What happened here?"

"Today we're burying five men killed by outlaws right here in town. The men you met with the coffin in their rig were taking the sixth dead man to his ranch to be buried. . .and I've got three more dead ones in my embalming shed. They were the outlaws."

Sheriff Hollister's grey eyes, set back under a heavy shelf of bone, looked steadily at Doc. "That's nine dead men, Doctor."

"Yes it is, Sheriff, I've got to get out there."

Ash Hollister agreed. "Yes. Just one more question: As the local medicine man you'd clean up corpses, so you'd know about such things as men gettin' killed around here."

Doc would have interrupted. As it was he was beginning to move when Sheriff Hollister spoke again.

"Mister Padgett put in for the bounty money on four fellers from up in my bailiwick. 'Horse-thieves,' Mister Padgett said in his letter. We're willin' to pay. In fact I got a draft for the full amount in my pocket. It's just that we want to make plumb certain. Their names were Frank Ballester, Fritz Hahn, Charley Simpson and Dick Arnett."

Doc stopped moving. "What was the last name again?"

"Dick Arnett. He didn't have much of a record, but lots of times all that means is that a feller hasn't been caught very often. He was a cowboy; a pretty good hand so they say. He had a wife and a little kid somewhere."

Doctor Winthrop stared at the massively built man who did not seem as tall as he was because of his width. Then he said, "Oh hell," in a tone

158

that rang with anguish.

Ash Hollister was watching him. "Somethin' wrong?"

Doc made a deaths-head smile. "Yeah. In fact Sheriff, nothing is right. Now I've got to go."

This time Doc did not stop. He did not look back either or he would have seen the curious, mildly perplexed expression on the big man's face.

The heat had been increasing since about noon and there was dust where Doc walked because of dozens of other people who had preceded him. Up ahead it was possible to see a large crowd milling around where Jim Danforth, sweating like a stud horse in his rusty old black coat and constricting black necktie, had just off-loaded the last pine box with the aid of several other men in black. They had the coffins sitting on sawhorses lined up to one side of each grave.

Sam Starr's leathery face was creased by a frown of concentration and his lips moved steadily as he read from his Bible, standing slightly apart in the shade of someone's top-buggy. He had done this often enough but still could not memorize anything.

There were three musicians, all long-standing patrons of Arley Patton's saloon. One played a fiddle, another one played a fife, and the third

one played a Jew's harp. They were making dis-
creet and discordant sounds behind Danforth's
hearse as they warmed up for the hymns they
would play after Sam's eulogies and sermon.

Doc had to halt to catch his breath before
starting to climb the broad, low hill. It was not
high at all and it was wide and flat on top but
he was breathless anyway.

He looked up there recognizing faces he saw
often and a lot more he saw only occasionally.
Marshal Padgett was there in black standing
beside Bessie Nevins who was also in black. It
did not become her, Doc thought. She was a
small, perfectly rounded woman, with eyes the
color of corn flowers, the kind of sweet-disposi-
tioned woman no man in his right mind would
abandon. Doc knew her story as well as anyone else did.

Jesus, the widow and the murderer of her
husband standing together made Doc want to
turn around and go back. Instead he hiked up
the hill and stood in hot sunlight gazing back
down in the direction of town. He did not even
hear Walt Nevins speak, so Walt walked away
as solemn as an owl to seek other company.

He was just beginning to understand something that sickened him. Padgett had told him
the reason he had not put the names on the
headboards of those four horsethieves was be-

cause he did not believe they deserved it. That was not the reason at all. Padgett also knew Bessie's story and the name of the cowboy who had abandoned her up in Wyoming.

Sam stepped up flush-faced. He fixed his eyes over everyone's head and spoke the few sentences he knew by heart, then ducked his head to start reading from his Bible. Now, all the talking died away.

Doc remained where he was, looking down from the hill in the direction of town. He was thinking of the big lawman from Wyoming and eventually he thought of something else. He had prepared those four dead horsethieves for burial and he remembered their faces perfectly, but because he had never learned their names he did not know which one had been Bessie's husband.

Maybe Arnett had not been the one who had run or the one who had thrown up his arms to surrender. Maybe Doc's feelings about Marshal Padgett were running away with him. He had to find out if the grey, lifeless face he remembered with the puckery little blue hole in the forehead had belonged to Arnett, or if the man with the hole in his back had been Arnett.

Sam was droning on and a little boy near Doc whose mother was gripping his hand like a vise, was squirming and squeezing his legs together, his freckled face reflecting pure anguish.

How, Doc asked himself, was he going to find out which one of those horsethieves had been Arnett?

14

The answer came effortlessly hours later when Doc was in his kitchen scrambling eggs and standing in his stocking feet. The ground had been so hot up on the hill that he'd been unable to move after services started and now his feet felt parboiled.

If Marshal Padgett had put in for bounty money on Arnett and the other horsethieves, he had done so after learning all about them. He would get that information from fugitive posters.

Doc slid the greasy egg onto a plate and took it to the table along with some hard bread and a pathetic-looking orange. That sheriff from Wyoming probably had brought dodgers on those four horsethieves with him. If he had brought a draft, he must also have brought copies of the dodgers.

It made Doc feel better to consider this. He had not felt very good throughout the services nor later when he had been dragooned — pulpy feet and all — to help shovel dirt into the graves.

He had considered going down to the cafe but the place would be three deep in hungry humanity and he had seen all the too-loose black coats that hung like sackcloth below lugubrious faces he could stand for one day. Besides, in the rare moments of his later life when he had needed someone to talk to, he would go out to the mantel and pour it all out to the fading portrait of his dead wife. She always smiled as encouragingly back at him as she had done in life from within the carved frame he had made himself, using an old scalpel which was good enough for wood but not good enough for the functions it had been manufactured for.

He finished his meal and dumped the dishes in a bucket of greasy water beside the stove. Unwilling for the moment to heat water and do them up properly, he padded out to light his parlor lamp and saw something in the roadway which drew him to a curtained window.

It was Jim Danforth's nicest little top-buggy, the one with a tassled fringe all around the upper top, being drawn by a big stud-necked seal brown mare. The passengers were Marshal Padgett and Bessie Nevins. Behind the seat where the rig was extended above the springs there was a picnic hamper on the floor.

Doc watched the buggy all the way up out of town northward. He then walked briskly back into the kitchen, mixed some whisky and water in a cup, and returned to the parlor. Holding the cup he stood in front of the handsome, gently smiling woman in her carved wooden frame on the mantel.

Doc was drinking coffee when someone arrived on the porch out front and rattled his door with a heavy fist. He sat long enough to finish it before going through the house to open the door. That massively built sheriff from Wyoming was standing there looking even more rumpled than he had looked yesterday. Without smiling he said, "Good morning. If you can spare a few minutes I'd like to talk to you."

Doc stepped back, then closed the door and led the way to his kitchen. He got a clean cup as he said, "Coffee?" The large man dropped his hat atop the table and nodded. Doc refilled his own cup and they sat down. The big man was pensive and quiet until Doc said, "Did you find Marshal Padgett?" then he looked steadily at Doc as he replied.

"Well, I saw him, but I didn't meet him." Hollister leaned down upon the table, thick shoulders hunched a little. "I had supper last night and got a room, then I did some thinking. The upshot was that I decided to come see you again."

Doc's third cup of coffee this morning tasted as bitter as original sin so he pushed the cup away. He squared around and said, "I'm glad you came by because since last evening I've wanted to ask you a question: By any chance do you have copies of the dodgers on those four horsethieves?"

The big man nodded his head. "You want to see them?"

"I'd like to, yes."

Sheriff Hollister remained motionless. "I have them in my pocket." He made no move to reach inside his coat but continued to sit there staring at Doc. "I'm not exactly sure about what is going on," he said in that very mild voice which did not fit the rest of him. "But after talkin' to you yesterday and takin' care of my horse, I killed a little time around town.... And later I went up to the cemetery lookin' for headboards."

Doc said, "And you found four that simply said Horsethief and gave the date they were killed."

Sheriff Hollister leaned back off the table. "That's right. I loafed around a little last night talkin' and listening."

166

Doc was a direct man and did not like disassemblers so he said, "Sheriff, we're goin' to be here all day unless you quit beating around the bush. Why don't you just spit it out?"

Ash Hollister's sunk-set grey eyes mirrored faint, hard humor. "I need someone who knows these folks to tell me whether some of the talk I heard last night is pure bull or not."

Doc held out a hand. "Let me see the dodgers."

Sheriff Hollister spread out the four posters with an air of gravity and Doc glanced at them all before fixing his attention upon a particular dodger. It bore the likeness of the horsethief who had been shot through the head while holding both arms in the air. Below the likeness was the man's name: Dick Arnett. Doc sounded more disillusioned or exasperated than angry when he said, "Damn it all anyway."

Sheriff Hollister's brows dropped a notch. "What's the trouble?"

Doc tapped the Arnett poster and told him who Arnett had been: The husband of the daughter of the storekeeper here in town, the father of a little boy called Jamie. Then, having said that much, in a bitter voice he also told Ash Hollister the reason Marshal Padgett had given him for not putting names on those headboards. Finally, he said, "Maybe that's true.

167

With a feller like Padgett there is an awful lot you can't be sure of, but he's got to know Bessie's last name. He's taken her buggy-riding. He knew her before he killed this man. I'll believe he had no idea who Arnett was until after he'd killed him, Sheriff, but afterward he damned well knew what their connection was and because he was sparkin' Bessie he deliberately didn't put Arnett's name on a headboard. . . . And yesterday he was up there with her at the burials, and last night he took her buggy riding."

Ash Hollister regarded his coffee cup with a solemn look. Maybe Marshal Padgett was a hypocrite. If so he sure as hell had no corner on that market. Moreover, none of this had anything to do with why Hollister was sitting in Doc's kitchen. Nor had Hollister met Marshal Padgett and he had learned years ago not to accept judgments made by other people. Eventually he raised his eyes to Doc's face and said, "I sympathize with what you folks down here may have on your hands, Doctor, but what I came by for this morning was to have you identify these four men as the ones Padgett brought in and you fixed up for burial. In other words I wanted a third party to confirm these are the men your town marshal brought in."

Doc looked dumbly at the bull-necked man, then reddened a little. He must have sounded like a gossip, an old granny. He straightened in the chair and looked stonily at the posters. "Yes, these are the four horsethieves Marshal Padgett brought in." Doc looked up. Right this minute he was feeling perverse. "And I have three more dead outlaws across the alley in my embalmin' shed if you'd like to see them. One shot in the back and one shot between the eyes like two of these other men — one with powder burns."

Sheriff Hollister fidgeted as he wordlessly picked up his four posters and dropped the hat atop his head while regarding Doctor Winthrop. "About all I can tell you," he said, "is that I won't mention any of this to Padgett when we meet." Hollister lumbered up to his feet, baggy coat hooked atop the handle of his holstered beltgun. He straightened the coat absentmindedly, still gazing at Doc. "I'm obliged for your help and I thank you for the coffee."

Doc arose nodding and trooped behind the much larger man to the parlor. Out there Sheriff Hollister leaned with a hand on the door latch for a moment before speaking again. "Those fellers in your shed," he said, and dropped his hand from the latch as he turned to face Doctor Winthrop. "Which one had powder burns?"

"The one shot between the eyes. Shot exactly as Arnett was shot, at close range facing Padgett. Arnett had both his hands in the air and he was unarmed when he was killed."

"Were you out there, Doctor? Did you see it?"

"No, I wan't out there, but some rangemen were and they saw how Marshal Padgett killed Arnett. As for the one in my shed, as nearly as I know no one saw the actual murder but some posse men from town saw the body moments later, and that man was also unarmed." Doc made a deaths-head smile. "Mister Hollister, I know this is not your bailiwick and you'd prefer not to buy into our troubles, but a year or so ago a cowboy named Cal Vincent — so damned drunk he couldn't find his butt with both hands — got involved in a ruckus at the saloon. Marshal Padgett walked in and shot him the same way, between the eyes from no farther off than the doorway."

Hollister stood there looking grave. "If all this is true, how does he get away with it?"

Doc looked sardonically at the lawman. "You haven't met him. When you have you may learn the answer to that, and Sheriff, as I told a friend of mine a while back before he died: It's not finished."

Ash Hollister walked out into the porch, reset his hat then hiked out through the gate and turned southward. Doc watched for a moment before retreating back to the kitchen where he heated water, did the dishes, and afterward got busy at other things.

Swen Jorgenson came by and they went out back together so Swen could measure the dead outlaws. He worked in silence; he was not a great talker at any time. When he had finished making notes he looked at Doc and said, "You see that one shot in the face? There's talk around town . . ."

Doc had not heard this before but he was not surprised because he had expected nothing less, sooner or later and evidently it was going to be sooner. "What talk?" he asked.

Swen was both elderly and prudent. He considered the corpses and even the open alley doorway before answering. "That one there, Doctor, the one shot in the face — didn't have no gun."

"Who told you that?"

Swen shook his head. "That don't matter. Anyway it's common talk. . . . I'll put together the coffins by tomorrow. When do you want to plant these three?"

"Tomorrow afternoon if someone will hire out to dig the graves," Doc replied as he herded the carpenter out into the alley so that he could lock the door.

It had been customary when grave diggers were needed to go among the loafers at Arley's saloon to recruit them. The alternative had been to see Marshal Padgett because in the past he had attended to such things.

Arley was gone, the saloon was padlocked, and Doc did what he had been avoiding for several days now: He went down to the jail-house.

Marshal Padgett saw him coming from a front-wall window where he had been standing in thought, smoking and watching the road-way. When Doc entered Marshal Padgett re-garded him from an expressionless face and motioned toward a chair as he went over to the desk. The marshal sat down and leaned back without taking his eyes off Doc, who was the man who, during a conversation last month after he'd settled with those horsethieves, had said something about the way two of them had been killed.

Last night Padgett had learned from the store-keeper's daughter that there was talk around town about the latest band of outlaws he had brought in. The talk was that a couple of them had been murdered by the marshal. This morn-ing Padgett was full of venom.

Doc did not meet the steady eyes. He fished around for his plug, worried off a corner, and got it pouched properly before he explained about the need for gravediggers. Then he looked

172

up. "Swen will have the boxes ready tomorrow. I think it'd ought to be taken care of no later than in the afternoon tomorrow. I mean the burials."

Marshal Padgett drew on his cheroot, removed it, and tapped off the ash. He ignored everything Doc had said. "Y'know, Doctor, in my job it's not like setting a busted arm or takin' a can of corn off a shelf for someone in a store."

Doc watched the tanned, handsome face and began to get a little dry in the throat.

Padgett plugged the stogie back between his teeth and spoke around it. "A place like Juniper hires a lawman because it don't have any choice. Mostly, because it don't have anyone with the guts to do what a lawman's got to do to keep order. It's a special kind of work an' calls for a special kind of man." Padgett paused to trickle smoke and for the first time to shift his gaze to the window and away from Doc as he went on speaking in a voice lacking both inflection and resonance.

"Like your work, Doctor, only more professional because I got the authority of life an' death. . . . You and Mister Nevins don't have to take any risks. I do. That's my job and I know how to do it." The blue eyes came slowly back to Doc's face. "I got a reputation to protect,

Doctor. . . . No one calls me a murderer."

Doc could feel sweat popping out beneath his shirt. His gaze was fixed on Marshal Padgett's face where the earlier lack of expression had subtly changed during the course of their visit. Doc made no effort to analyze the expression now because he felt certain that Sheriff Hollister had not kept his word and had told Marshal Padgett what Doc had said over coffee in his kitchen, and that worried him more than anything else.

But evidently he was wrong because Padgett said, "Those fellers who went down there from town to lend me a hand runnin' those sons of bitches to ground. . . they stopped half a mile out and let me fight it out with the odds at three to one. Then they came back to town and commenced saying I didn't give those outlaws a chance."

Doc twisted to expectorate out the doorway and across the plankwalk into the road. As he squared back around, Marshal Padgett rose and went to the wood stove for a cup of coffee. He offered one to Doc who declined and watched Padgett return to his chair. "People talk," Doc said. "When there isn't anything to gossip about they make up something."

Marshal Padgett seemed not to hear. He leaned with both hands curled around the cup.

174

"Logan," he said quietly. "That redheaded feller who swamped around the smithy for Mister Myser. He has been talking against me. Him and a hostler who works up at the corralyard. Maybe the others, too, but I suspicion those two most of all."

Doc spread his hands. "Not Will Logan, Marshal. I've known him ever since he came to town to work for Don Myser. He is a quiet young man. I've never heard him gossip."

Because Marshal Padgett sat motionless cupping his coffee mug in both hands looking past Doc at the wall, it seemed to Doc to be a good moment to get off this subject, so he mentioned the need for gravediggers again. The only response he got was that Marshal Padgett leaned back in his chair and absently nodded.

Doc tried another tack. "There was a Wyoming sheriff around town lookin' for you. Name is Hollister, by any chance did you meet him?"

This time the response was more than a nod. "Yeah. He was in a while back. He was interested in these horsethieves. I showed him the dodgers and the junk I took out of their pockets and he said he'd had a long ride, was tired, and he'd come back later." Padgett's mood seemed to be veering back to normal but Doc scarcely noticed. Hollister had evidently refrained from mentioning that he had a draft to cover the bounty money and he had not been tired in Doc's kitchen. In fact he had arrived yesterday not today and had presumably bedded down at the rooming house last night so he would have been fresh enough this morning.

Doc's curiosity was up like a flag, but he allowed the topic to die. He rose and said, "About those gravediggers . . ."

Marshal Padgett leaned as though to also rise. "I'll take care of that. There is always someone around."

Doc walked back out into the sunshine. Across the road Walt Nevins and a younger man who, Doc speculated, might be old Angus's replacement as store clerk, were going over a tally of supplies for a rough-looking cowman from east of town named Bud Hampstead. Doc knew him from having delivered a baby from his wife a couple of years back. They exchanged a wave.

As he went past the harness works Sam appeared in the doorway with some thread in one hand, a ball of beeswax in the other hand. He watched Doc approach while pulling the twisted strands of thread through the wax. Sam smiled, "Swen told me them outlaws are due to get buried tomorrow afternoon. Is that right?"

It was. "Yeah, I just talked to the marshal.

He's going to round up the diggers. It'll be up to you about praying over them."

Sam continued to wax his thread and regard Doctor Winthrop. "If you got a minute, Doc, come inside."

It was cooler in the shop. Cooler and poorly lighted. Sam Starr put aside the wax and ran both big, callused hands down the front of his apron. He was a large, rawboned older man with a face blasted out of a life of hardship. He was not talkative nor did he smile a lot. He did not smile now as he said, "A stranger come in this morning lookin' to get some sewing done on a bridle." Sam pointed to a headstall hanging from a nail. "Lost his buckle off the throat latch. He'll be along directly...built like a bear."

Doc, who was beginning to get impatient, narrowed his eyes at Sam's description.

"When he bent down to pick up somethin' he'd dropped, Doc, some folded papers fell out of his pocket. They was dodgers. I picked 'em to hand them back and looked at the top one."

There was a slight noise in the doorway behind Doc which he ignored as the harness maker went on speaking.

"It was for a horsethief named Dick Arnett wanted up north. This big feller taken the posters back to pocket them and said this

177

Arnett-feller was one of the horsethieves Marshal Padgett killed last month. Doc, the name stuck in my craw because..."

There was a louder noise from the doorway and both men turned. Walt Nevins's daughter was lying in a heap where she had fainted.

15

Doc didn't have much appetite, but he made a stew and set it to simmer while he slumped at the kitchen table.

Even after he and Sam Starr had revived Bessie she had not acted rational. They took her home and the moment she was inside the house she started to scream. The harness maker had been badly shaken. Doc took her through the house to a bedroom and pushed her down upon the bed. She rolled over, buried her face in the quilt, and began to cry.

Doc returned to the parlor, took Sam in tow, and they departed. He sent Sam to tell Walt what had happened, then went after his satchel, and returned to mix some sleeping powder into water and make Bessie drink it. Afterward, when he was leaving the house, he encountered Walt. Doc brushed on by without a word.

Lately he had been drinking more than he should so he had slackened off. But now as he sat in the kitchen the need arose, so he filled a cup and nursed it while waiting for his supper to cook.

Someone knocking on the door brought Doc back to the present. He went out front. It was Walt Nevins and he looked as though he had aged fifteen years this afternoon. Wordlessly Doc took him back to the kitchen, poured another cupful, and placed it in front of a chair at the table. "Sit down," he said.

Walt sat. He ignored the cup and somewhat absently polished his glasses. After a while he said, "Didn't you or Sam see her standing there?"

Doc took that as an accusation. "We were talking. I wasn't thinking about anything except what Sam was saying. What the hell was she doing at the harness works anyway?"

"Jamie... the gunbelt she gave him got ripped when he was climbing a tree and she took it over for Sam to sew up." For a moment the storekeeper eyed the cup, then reached for it. "It's hard to believe, Paul. I just can't believe Marshal Padgett knew who Arnett was."

Doc went to stir the stew, and while standing at the stove he told himself bleakly that the reason it was hard for Walt to believe was because he had always defended Padgett. Being wrong was hard any time. "I don't think he did know, until after he'd killed him and got the things from his pockets," he said.

"But...that's not what I mean, Doc. I mean — did he know when he was sparkin' my daughter? When they went buggy-riding and all, did he know it was her husband he had killed?"

Doc buried his snout in the cup and half-drained it. Of course he had known. He put the cup down. "How is she? I put her to sleep but that medicine wears off."

"Terrible," Nevins replied in a half whisper. "Too many things have happened to her this past year or so. She's — she trusts people, sees the best in them." Walt's eyes, watery behind his glasses, looked to Doc's face. "She almost never mentioned Arnett, but I think she still cared for him. She was hurt, most of all she was bewildered, just could not understand why he had abandoned her and Jamie. I wish to gawd her mother was alive."

Doc looked away from the crumpled face and gruffly said, "Finish your whisky," then returned to the stove. While he was standing there a heavy hand rattled his front door. He turned exasperatedly. "Drink it down, Walt. I'll be right back."

This time the caller was Sheriff Hollister,

181

recognizable even in the dark by his massive silhouette. Doc squinted at him then shrugged and stepped aside. "The storekeeper and I were sittin' in the kitchen. Come along."

Hollister stopped Doc with a hand on the shoulder. "I heard about his daughter when I went back to the harness works for my bridle."

Doc got from beneath the big hand and considered the large man a little coldly. "You bought in when you dropped those damned dodgers whether you want to or not, Sheriff. And tell me something: Why didn't you tell Marshal Padgett you had his bounty money for him; why did you beat around the bush with him?"

Hollister's sunk-set eyes did not blink in his gaze at the older, shorter, and much slighter man. "Where I come from they don't very often pay for murder, Doctor. I know I sure as hell don't. I wanted to ask around and see if your views are just your own or the views of other folks too."

"And?" enquired Doc acidly.

"It was a little like talkin' to a stone wall... except for a couple of fellers. One of them is a rancher I met about a half hour ago. Feller named Mitch Smith."

"What did he say?"

"Quite a bit," stated the big man with the

mild voice. "I met him before. The day I first arrived. He and another feller were driving a wagon with a coffin in back. He remembered me too."

"Did you tell him who you are — a lawman from up north?"

"Well, I sort of had to. I didn't figure on it but he's not real talkative and when I got to askin' questions he didn't much like it, so I told him. After that he talked all right. Seems the man in the coffin was his boss and he was pretty bitter about his gettin' shot down, and pretty bitter about some other things."

"About how Marshal Padgett brought in the men who had killed his employer?"

"Yes."

Doc looked down, then up. "We were having some whisky in the kitchen. You can join us if you care to." He did not look around to see whether the invitation had been accepted or not, he just started walking.

Marshal Hollister followed.

In the kitchen Doc introduced them and Walt's eyes widened as he shook the sheriff's hand. He said, "You're the lawman from Wyoming?"

Hollister nodded, sat down, and dropped his hat on the floor beside the chair.

Walt started talking, words poured out. Doc

handed Hollister a cup of watered whisky and met the sheriff's quizzical look with a barely discernible shrug. Whether Hollister knew it or not what Walt was doing was getting the load off his chest. When he had told all that he knew, Walt asked a question of Ash Hollister.

"I met Arnett once, the day he married my daughter. After that they left for Wyoming. Tell me straight out, Sheriff: Was he an outlaw?"

Hollister shot Doc a sidelong glance before answering. "He did a few things. Nothing that deserved getting shot about until he came down here with his running mates to steal horses. . . . If you mean, had he used a gun, I guess I can tell you that he hadn't. He wasn't a killer. In fact, from what I know about him, Mister Nevins, he wouldn't put up a real battle with the law."

Hollister tasted the drink. It was strong enough to melt the *cajones* off a brass monkey. He put it aside and regarded Nevins for a long, thoughtful moment then asked a question of his own. "Did your daughter know he was down here?"

Walt shook his head. "She didn't. She had no idea where he was. He never wrote. I think that's partly what upset her so bad. His being here, close enough at least to ride in and see

184

their son. But . . ."

Both the other men were watching Nevins, silent and motionless.

"But the way Marshal Padgett did this." Walt's eyes came up again, dark with anguish. "He took her buggy-riding. She made up food for them and all. He held her arm up at Cemetery Hill during the burials. She refuses to talk to me about him. Something happened to her today when she overheard the harness maker and Doctor Winthrop talking. Marshal Padgett knew he had killed her husband an' he still took her buggy-riding and all. . . . She was . . . He's a handsome man and all. Bessie's been alone a long while now." The voice trailed off.

Doc broke this up. "Sheriff, what about the bounty money?"

Hollister eyed the cup as he answered, seeming to pick the words carefully. "I'm up against something I've never run into before, gents. I been a peace officer twelve years and figured I'd seen it all." He looked away from the cup but did not raise his eyes. "He got them; he earned the rewards."

Doc snorted.

That brought the grey eyes up. "I'm not a fee lawyer nor a judge." Hollister blew out a long breath. "Like I already said, where I come from they don't pay for murder. . . . But maybe . . .

Only that's just part of it. As near as I can count, your town marshal has killed eight men over the past year or so. Four horsethieves, three store robbers and a cowboy. One was too drunk to know what was happening and two was shot between the eyes when they weren't armed. I guess to answer your question, Doctor, I got to say no, I'm not going to hand over the bounty-money draft. I'm goin' to write to the governor of my state an' ask him to write the governor of your state to have someone come in here and investigate all the things that've happened here. I don't know what else to do."

For ten seconds there was absolute silence, then the muffled sound of a gunshot rattled some windows in the front of Doc's house. For all his size the sheriff from Wyoming moved fast. He was off his chair and through the door leading from the kitchen before either Nevins or Doctor Winthrop had recovered from their astonishment.

Out front the roadway was eerily lighted by a soaring moon. There were a few lights among the business buildings on both sides of Main Street, and except for a few tethered saddle animals at the tie-racks that were shifting nervously in the wake of that thunderous muzzle-blast, there was no movement at all. Doc and Walt reached the gate in time to hear two men shouting down near the corralyard. Sheriff Hollister was striding in that direction.

Doc started to follow but Walt grabbed him.. "Don't go down there," he exclaimed.

Doc jerked free and went anyway. The stage company office had light showing through the front window and the corralyard gates were wide open, which they normally were. Doc could make out a tall man standing in the gate opening facing the roadway.

He could also see the unmistakable silhouette of the massive lawman from Wyoming as he got down there and halted. He and the tall man seemed to exchange a few words then the sheriff entered the yard.

By the time Doc reached the opening the tall man was strolling southward, but Doc recognized him finally, and with a bitter taste in his throat he too entered the corralyard.

Four men were standing in a rough circle, two with lanterns. Ash Hollister blocked Doc's view until he got up close enough to circle around and see the sprawled body outlined in the dust by wavery lamplight.

No one objected as Doc pushed through and knelt. He knew the corralyard man only by sight; he had been working for the stage company about a year. He was some kind of a 'breed, perhaps part Indian or part Mexican. The bullet which had ended his life had struck him above the eyes in the middle of the forehead. He was still warm and blood was leaking from his wound, but the man had been dead before he had stopped rolling. There were powder burns.

One of the hostlers leaned above Doc, his lantern making shifting patterns as it swayed. The man seemed about to speak but his mouth remained open with no words coming out as he saw the thumb-sized hole. He straightened back.

Doc turned the head to examine the bullet's exiting hole, then he gently eased the head down and raised his eyes to Sheriff Hollister. He was stonily regarding the dead man so their eyes did not meet.

A breathless individual came rushing in from out front as Doc got stiffly to his feet. The newcomer, who owned the stage company franchise for Piute Valley and surrounding areas, stopped in his tracks when he saw the dead man.

Doc wiped both hands on a handkerchief and turned his back to walk away. Bitterness filled him. He was unaware of someone taking long strides behind him until they came together out near the gateway and the Wyoming lawman said, "Fair fight."

Doc turned slowly.

Hollister held out an old six-gun. "It was

beneath him. One of the other hostlers saw it happen. The dead man went for his gun."

Doc's face contorted. "Went for his gun? Are you blind or crazy? He couldn't have beaten Marshal Padgett if he'd already had his damned gun up and pointed."

Hollister let the gun hang at his side and glanced southward through the ghostly doom. "Why this one, Doctor?"

"Because he was one of the men from town who went down south when Marshal Padgett chased those men who robbed the store. They saw the men Padgett had killed and when they got back, they started talking about it. They said it was murder. That's why."

When Doc got back to the gate of his house Walt Nevins was gone. He went to the kitchen, picked up the cup Sheriff Hollister had barely touched, and drank its contents.

The stew water had boiled away. What remained of his supper looked like a collection of uniformly black, misshapen stones in the bottom of the pot. Doc took the pot out back and left it there.

Juniper was so quiet that when the southbound coach hauled down to a walk before entering town from the north, Doc distinctly heard the rattle of tug chains, shod hooves, and steel tires grinding roadway grit into fine powder.

He left the house and went out to stand in moonlight and summer warmth in his rear yard where weeds flourished but where he had once raised a vegetable garden. It was utterly peaceful out there. Doc sat on an up-ended horseshoe keg and put his face in his hands.

16

The town had been making a genuine — but slow — effort to recover since the burials out at Cemetery Hill. The day after the killing of Mike Barney, the corralyard hostler, a fresh element was noticeable to Doctor Winthrop. Fear.

The cafeman's widow, for example, had been bitterly outspoken. Now she did not open her mouth.

There were others. The rooming house proprietor who, like Walt Nevins and others around town who had defended Marshal Padgett, abruptly began staying to himself and refusing to discuss anything that had happened lately, even with Dr. Winthrop.

Swen Jorgenson, when summoned to Doc's shed to take measurements of the corralyard man, refused to discuss what had happened when Doc brought the subject up. Swen did what he had come to do — put up his measuring tape and start working away. He stopped a moment in the doorway to look at Doc and wag his head, then he departed in silence.

Marshal Padgett arrived at Doc's front door in the early morning of the following day, and when Doc admitted him a knot formed somewhere behind his belt. Padgett took a chair, carefully balanced his handsome beaver-belly hat on the knee of a crossed leg, and said, "He tried to draw on me." The lawman's dark blue eyes remained fixed upon Doc's face.

It was a short, difficult struggle for Doc. Prudence lost out. In a bitter tone the medical practitioner returned Jack Padgett's look and sat down. "Marshal, if old Pruitt, the man you took over from, had got into an argument with someone like Barney, he'd have knocked him down or maybe at the very worst, hit him over the head and dragged him down to be locked up."

Padgett's eyes did not waver from Doc's face. "You weren't there, Doctor. He was spoiling for a fight and went for his gun. No one in his right mind would try to rush a man to knock him down under those circumstances. He was drawing."

Doc kept the indignation damned up behind

192

his teeth and simply sat there looking at the tall, handsome man in his ironed shirt and carved belt and holster.

Padgett loosened slightly. Some of the hardness left his face. "I'm goin' to tell you exactly what happened because I know folks come to you like they'd do to a preacher. . . . I was outside the corralyard gate, just standin' there, when Barney crossed the yard behind me. I heard him and faced around. He said something. I didn't catch it so I asked him to repeat it. . . . He went for his gun."

Doc stared at the town marshal. "Where was he, halfway back in the yard, Marshal?"

Padgett shrugged with indifference. "Yeah, . halfway back. That's why I couldn't hear what he said."

Doc forced his eyes to the hands lying limply in his lap. The distance from the gate to the middle of the yard was no less than thirty feet, perhaps forty-five feet. Marshal Padgett was lying. Until that other hostler had leaned above him, Doc had been unable to see the powder burns because Mike Barney had a dark complexion. By lampglow, however, they were easily reconizable. A man did not have powder burns on his face when he had been shot from forty-five feet away. Padgett had been much closer.

Doc raised his head. "Well, Swen came by for measurements and I suppose we can bury Barney this afternoon when we bury the others." He got to his feet and Marshal Padgett did the same. As he put on his hat he said, "I wanted you to know, Doctor."

Doc nodded and held the door for Padgett to depart. Afterward he closed it softly. There had been five men in the group that had raced out of town in the marshal's wake to help him run down the store robbers. Now there were four. Doc went to a chair.

Yesterday Marshal Padgett had told him his reputation was at stake. Last night he had killed one of the five men who had been in that town posse. Doc thought of the redheaded blacksmith's helper, Will Logan, the young man with a troubled conscience. He was one of four survivors. Doc went to bed knowing what he had to do in the morning, and on his way out of the house after breakfast he scooped up his satchel along with his hat.

He did not want to face Bessie but he had a professional obligation to walk down to the Nevins' house. Walt was there, evidently he had decided not to go down to the store today. He admitted Doc and looked over his shoulder in the direction of the hallway as he spoke in a muted voice. "She's not much better...."

194

Paul, my daughter is like a little girl in some ways. She's vulnerable. She don't see evil in folks. You understand?"

Doc understood and it irritated him to hear Walt talk like this, because Doctor Winthrop had known Bessie almost as long as her father had. Right now he thought he probably understood Bessie's kind of a person better than her father did. But his response was controlled. "I brought some more sleepin' powder. You can administer them, Walt, but only when she'd ready for bed. The rest of the time she's going to have to get along without it." He dug in his satchel and held the small bottle for a moment before passing it over. "This stuff isn't a crutch, you understand? We don't want her to get to rely on it." He handed over the bottle.

Nevins took it and while examining it he said, "What happened last night?"

Winthrop snapped the satchel closed with finality. He did not want to discuss the corral-yard killing. "A yardman for the stage company got himself killed." Doc went to the door, nodded curtly and departed.

As he reached the far corner and turned, a lounging figure greeted him dryly. " 'Morning." With a start Doc recognized Mitch Smith. Smith had never been a frequent visitor to town, and it was now only a little past ten o'clock in the morning, which was early for any of the outlying cowmen to be in town except for an emergency. Clearly this was not one because Mitch Smith had one booted foot on the store wall at his back and the rest of his body relaxed in a slouch.

Doc squinted. His feeling was that this was not an accidental encounter. He said, " 'Morning. You must have got up before breakfast." It was a long ride from the Macklin place to Juniper.

Mitch's bronzed faced was blank except for the slight squint up around his eyes. "Heard about the killing last night," he said quietly. "A Patterson rider came by on his way back from town."

Doc said nothing.

Mitch Smith straightened up off the wall and idly glanced southward toward the distant lower end of town. There was not a soul in sight except for a woman coming out of Nevins's store with a full shopping basket on her arm. Mitch looked back at Doc. He was a direct individual, a very practical, sensible man. He said, "I think someone had better put an end to this, Doctor."

It required a little time for Doc to understand the meaning of this quiet statement. He stared at the younger, huskier man in the old faded range attire with the equally as worn and scratched holster low on his right side. "Tell me what you mean by that, Mitchell."

"Burt Standish and I talked a little last week when we had old Jeremiah's funeral at the ranch. Too many killings, Doctor. Too many that wasn't right. Then that one last night." The dead-level eyes regarded Doc steadily. "Folks don't want to talk about it, but I figured you'd know bein' the one who lays them out and all."

Doc moved closer to the storefront under the wooden overhang. "I see. And this wasn't an accidental meeting was it?"

"No. I saw you headin' for the Nevins house and decided to wait. I heard about that too; the marshal killin' her husband and hidin' it from her and the storekeeper."

Doc's irritability came up. "You've been busy this morning," he said sarcastically. "You said folks won't talk, but someone sure as hell must have."

Mitch ignored the sarcasm. "I said they wouldn't talk about what happened at the corralyard. Doctor, we've been in this country a long time, we got friends in town too."

Doc could have asked how Mitch knew what he thought only he, Bessie, her father and Marshal Padgett knew, but he refrained. It did not really matter anyway how Mitchell Smith knew about Arnett; probably by now the whole damned town knew. The best way to keep something private in a place like Juniper was to tell it first.

Doc sighed in silence. "All I can tell you about the corralyard killing is that Marshal Padgett shot a hostler named Mike Barney."

"I knew him. How did he shoot him?"

"Between the eyes," said Doc, having trouble with the words.

"Fair fight was it?" asked the stockman, showing a skepticism in his expression. "Like hell it was."

Doc saw Sheriff Hollister emerge from the harness shop onto the far plankwalk southward. Hollister glanced northward, saw them standing in the shade and stared without embarrassment before turning to stroll in the direction of the jailhouse.

Jim Danforth emerged from the saloon, which surprised Doc because the doors had been padlocked after Arley Patton's death. Jim walked southward too, but on the opposite side of Main Street.

Smith spoke again. "I'd like to know the details of the killing last night, Doctor."

"I told you what I know," retorted Doc, straightening up off the store wall. He reconsidered that, then also said, "Listen to me..."

"I'm listening."

Doc looked at the strong, rather handsome face of the stockman and wanted to swear long and loud. Instead he picked his words. "You and Burt think that riding into town loaded for bear will resolve everything, do you?"

Smith gave a delayed, slow response to that. "Doctor, as near as we can see, you folks here in town aren't goin' to do anything until there's none of you left. Why would he walk into the corralyard and shoot a man down he barely even knew?"

"Mitchell—"

"Let me finish, Doctor. I told you before he did right goin' after those men who blew up Mister Nevins's safe and shot Jeremiah. But not murder... Doctor, Burt and I and our riders saw him do that twice. Kill men like they was wolves. No chance at all, just shot them dead. Last night it had to be about the same. Tomorrow or the next day it'll be you or Danforth or Nevins." Smith gazed southward. "Burt will be along later. My riders will be along directly too." He was watching the front of the distant jailhouse. "It may not be your way of settling this, but it's our way."

Doctor Winthrop was sweating. It was indeed a warm day, but under the overhang it wasn't. He could visualize it: rangemen coming down

199

Main Street, the fight that would follow, windows being shot out, people hiding in terror, perhaps some of them being injured — and maybe this man at his side dead along with other stockmen and Marshal Padgett.

He pulled down a shaky breath. "No," he exclaimed, facing the rangeman. "It's not going to be done that way."

"How then?"

Doc had no idea and he did not like being pushed into this. "I don't know, but not your way," he said, glaring. Then he turned southward gripping his satchel, his eyes fixed upon the blacksmith shop on the same side of the road and a few doors south of the jailhouse.

By the time he reached the smithy his shirt was wringing wet front and back. He badly needed a drink — water, this time — which he got from the bucket and dipper inside the sooty blacksmith shop. Redheaded Will Logan was heating bar steel to make horseshoe blanks out of, something which was normally done at a smithy when there was slack time.

Logan eyed Doc while keeping up his slow, rhythmic pumping of the bellows. The forge had cherry-red oak knots instead of coal or coke in it and the bar steel matched that color as Logan alternately watched it and Doctor Winthrop. Finally he gave the bellows handle an extra pump and with an annoyed expression put the bar aside. He would have to do all this over again after Doc departed.

He wiped his face and arms, strolled over near the bucket and said, "I know. You've come to warn me."

That was exactly why Doc had come. But it was not the only reason. "Not just you, the other three. But I have to first know who they are."

Logan's sweat-shiny face showed sardonic amusement. "They're gone, Doctor. Left town this morning before sunup. I guess it didn't take them any longer'n it took me to figure out why Mike Barney was egged into a fight he couldn't win."

"You're sure they're gone?"

"I'm sure, Doctor. They came to see me last night and figured I'd better go with them."

"Why didn't you?"

Logan shrugged. "Too dumb I guess." He refused to expand on that but there was a look in his eyes that contradicted it. He was not the fleeing kind.

Logan then said something that surprised Doctor Winthrop. "He didn't give Mike Barney a chance. He waited out front in the dark until Mike was crossin' the yard toward the bunk-house then called him. . . . He walked right up

201

to Mike, told him to hand over his gun. Mike started to lift it from the holster and Marshal Padgett shot him between the eyes."

Doc looked for something to sit on that was not completely covered with soot. "How do you know that's how it happened?"

"Because a feller called Slim Sommers was back there near a stagecoach that was blocked up with all four wheels off. Saw everything and heard everything. I guess Padgett didn't see him lookin' from behind the stage. . . . Afterward Padgett walked back out as far as the gateway and stood there with a damned cigar until folks come running."

Doc could not find anything to sit on. "Where is Sommers?"

Will Logan's wide mouth drew back in a mirthless grin. "Gone. He left town last night with the other fellers. He said he didn't think Padgett had seen him but he knew damned well what would happen to him if Padgett had, so he run. You can't blame a man for that."

Doc raised a limp handkerchief to mop at perspiration on his face. "Do you own a horse?" he asked and before all the words were out the young redheaded man was shaking his head. "Yeah I own a horse, but I'm not going to tuck tail and run."

"You're being foolish, Will."

202

"I guess so."

Logan's light blue eyes remained on Doc's face. Doc put away the handkerchief. There was nothing more to be said. Logan was one of those utterly stubborn people who could be dragged behind wild horses and still not change his mind. "Well, son," he said, "be careful. Don't turn your back to the doorway and if he comes over—"

"Doctor," the younger man interrupted, pointing. "See that shotgun? I can watch the jailhouse from here. The minute that son of a bitch starts from there to here. . . . See that carbine near the back door and the six-gun on the nail over yonder?" Logan dropped the arm back to his side. "I'll give him the same chance he gave Mike Barney and them fellers down south in the rocks."

17

The morning southbound coach raised dust north of town as the driver hauled his hitch down to a walk for the balance of the way. Farther back Doc saw more dust rising and halted with a hand on his gate to study it. Another man was looking back up there from up near the corner of the main thoroughfare. Doc saw him too and tightened his grip on the gate a little. It was Mitchell Smith and obviously he had been killing time in anticipation of that oncoming dust banner.

Doc did not move until a mild, deep voice spoke from up on his porch where Sheriff Ash Hollister was sitting in shadow.

"You see an In'ian war party, Doctor?"

Before replying Doc went up to the porch and eyed the large man speculatively. "No, I was watching a fairly big mob of rangemen.

You see that husky young feller up yonder across the road? That's your friend Mitchell Smith, and unless my eyesight is worse than I think it is, that cloud of dust far northward is his riders from the Macklin place, along with a man named Burt Standish from Patterson ranch with his riding crew. Altogether maybe eight or ten men are coming to town to kill Marshal Padgett."

Doc stepped to a rickety cane-bottomed chair and sat down to watch the dust. It was a long way off, which meant the rangemen would probably not reach town for another hour and a half or longer unless they busted over into a lope.

The Wyoming lawman was squinting northward from beneath the lowered flat brim of his hat. "Is that a fact," he said mildly. "Vigilantes, Doctor?"

That designation did not appeal much to Doctor Winthrop even though it was perhaps deserved. He told Hollister what Mitch Smith had said to him about settling things and Hollister got more comfortable in his chair while watching the distant dust. "I don't believe they'd ought to try it," he said mildly. "I was down there with the marshal for a while this morning. He was loading the weapons in his wall rack.... No, I don't think he's expecting anything like this, but he's not a man to take unnecessary chances. Like last night."

Doc faced around. Hollister was gazing stonily at him. "I made a mistake," the big man said. "It wasn't a fair fight." He jutted his chin in the direction of the dust. "If I make another guess I don't think I'll be wrong this time. Marshal Padgett forted up in that jailhouse will massacre those cowboys. He don't miss. I've yet to see a cowboy who could hit the side of a barn from the inside with his first couple of shots."

Doc was still watching the dust, feeling troubled and helpless, when Danforth's hearse came up through town and turned off in the direction of Cemetery Hill. He had quite forgotten the burials slated for this afternoon, but now he switched his attention and watched the handsome vehicle behind Jim's nice pair of blacks. He then leaned to crane down Main Street.

There was no sign of people as there had been for the earlier funeral, but he had not expected any, except perhaps for the sloe-eyed, dusky-skinned widow of Mike Barney and perhaps a couple of hostlers from the corralyard. What he searched for and did not see was Sam Starr in black with his off-side coat pocket sagging. Sam evidently was in no hurry; this was Danforth's first trip up there, he had three more trips to make, and it was a hot afternoon.

Sheriff Hollister arose and reset his hat, then nodded to Doc and strolled off.

Doc had a feeling of futility, of desperation. *He* could not stop what was in the making. He owned a gun but had not worn it in seven or eight years. Even if he got it now he was not sure that would do any good. One more damned gun was not going to be the answer; there were already too many guns.

He looked across the road but Sheriff Hollister was not in sight. He looked up yonder where the dust banner was closer, then squinted over under the wooden awning where Mitch Smith had been loafing for almost two hours now. Then he went after his hat and crossed the road with determined strides and when Smith saw him approaching, he shoved back his hat and waited, expressionless but obviously determined.

Doc said, "Listen to me — the last time Jeremiah and I talked at the ranch I told him something had to be done."

Smith nodded slowly. "I know that. You were right."

"But—"

"Doctor, it's too damned bad you didn't follow through on that because since then that son of a bitch has killed more men — and old Jeremiah is dead too."

"Jeremiah's killing can't be layed to Marshal Padgett, but that's beside the point. . . . Is that Burt Standish with his crew and your men?"

"Yes."

"Mitchell, don't try it. That big man who was with me on the porch a while back—"

"The lawman from Wyoming — Hollister."

"Yes, Sheriff Hollister, he told me that if you try to get Marshal Padgett, he can fort up in the jailhouse and turn our roadway into a slaughter ground. He's got all his weapons in there loaded and ready."

Mitch Smith turned his face northward where it was now possible to count the horsemen. "He's not goin' to get a chance to fort up, Doctor."

Danforth's hearse came down into town moving southward for its next coffin. Jim's big fleshy body turned slightly on the seat. He eyed Doctor Winthrop without a nod. Down in front of the stage company corralyard three men were standing like crows neither speaking nor moving as they watched the hearse pass along. Two of them were hostlers, the third one was the nervous, skinny man who ran the stage company in Piute Valley.

Marshal Padgett emerged from the jailhouse

and crossed the road behind the hearse to stand in front of the general store with a cigar between his teeth and his black holster with the contrasting ivory grips of his six-gun showing brightly in the sunshine.

Mitch turned back facing Doc. "We're just goin' to take our time and spread out around town. . . . Get between him and the jailhouse."

Doc furrowed his brow. "He's no novice, Mitchell. I've watched him for years. He don't miss anything that happens in the roadway. And by now he sure as hell suspects the cattlemen aren't his friends any more if they ever were. . . . the saloon isn't open for business, so why would so many rangemen be arriving in town — especially in the middle of the week?"

Smith said. "We don't much care what he thinks. Doctor, we got a lot of respect for you, for most of the folks here in town. But we've lost some good men too, and we're different from you. We don't expect to just set around and let things slide."

"That's what you did out yonder when you saw him deliberately shoot down two unarmed horsethieves. You did nothing. Mitchell, a pitched battle may take care of Marshal Padgett, but what about you and Burt and your riders, and maybe some innocent people here in town?"

Smith considered Doctor Winthrop for a long

time before speaking again. "All right," he said, ready to say more but Danforth's hearse was coming again, still at a slow walk, and this second trip held Smith's attention until the vehicle had gone past. "All right, Doctor. I'll tell you what we'll do. Put up the horses and loaf down in Danforth's barn so's you townspeople can do it yourselves. . . . A half hour, Doctor. . . . Then we'll do it."

Smith walked away heading up toward the area where the Juniper plankwalk ended north of town beside the roadway.

Doc stood looking helplessly down the nearly empty roadway. Marshal Padgett was no longer in sight. Logan, down at the blacksmith shop, started working at the anvil again, and this time the measured ringing put Doctor Winthrop in mind of church bells for a funeral. He entered the general store and saw Walt polishing his glasses. Only Walt and his new clerk were in there. Normally this time of day there were customers, now there were none. Walt hooked his spectacles into place and owlishly eyed the medical man as Doc went up and said, "I don't know that it will do any good, Walt, but you'd better call a meeting of the town council. You're chairman this year and—"

"Who do I call?" asked Nevins. "Don and Arley?"

That annoyed Doc. "Don't be silly. Jim's on the council this year, so am I and so are you. So is Sam Starr, but you'd better hurry or he'll be on his way out to the cemetery."

Nevins glanced out the front window. There was no one in sight across the road. He could see the jailhouse; the door was half open. He began to gently shake his head. "I . . . it wouldn't do any good. What should we do, fire him? Who's goin' to tell him that he's been fired by the town council? I'm not." Walt lowered his voice. "He bought three boxes of shells this morning, two for six-guns and one for Winchesters. . . . And he looked right through me, Paul." Nevins leaned a little and lowered his voice almost to a whisper. "Let it happen. My new hired man said he'd heard that the Patterson and Macklin riders are comin' to town today to settle with him for that cowboy he killed — Cal Vincent. . . . Paul, have you any idea what he's done to my daughter?"

Doc did not reply, nor did he move his gaze from the storekeeper's face. *He was too late,* but perhaps even if he'd tried to organize the town earlier, or even yesterday, it still would have been too late. People were afraid of Marshal Padgett; they wanted him killed but they were too afraid of him to do anything themselves, and now, because they knew the rangemen were

211

coming, they were like Walt Nevins — willing to remain out of sight and let the rangemen do it for them.

Doc left the store. He stopped out front. Marshal Padgett and Sheriff Hollister were standing over in front of the jailhouse under the overhang quietly talking. Doc's gaze lingered longest on the bearlike law officer from Wyoming. It had not occurred to him until this moment that Ash Hollister might have decided to side with Jack Padgett. He told himself his imagination was running away with him; Hollister was the man who had sat in Doc's waiting room saying he would not hand over the bounty money to a murderer, or something like that. And he's said other things.

Doc shifted his glance and watched Danforth coming back southward for his third trip. Jim was slouching on the seat, his face was sweat-shiny and the black plug hat he wore for funerals had been tipped to shield his eyes from sunglare as far as Jim could tip it without having it fall off.

Doc walked down as far as the smithy and stopped in the doorway. Will Logan was scrubbing at the water trough out back. Hanging from a nail was a pair of slightly green black trousers with a coat to match. There was even a black string tie and a moderately clean white shirt.

212

Logan looked up through dripping water, then resumed his ablutions. When he was finished and was drying off he said, "Was that Danforth's third or fourth trip?"

"Third. He's got one more trip after this one." Doc was eyeing the black coat and trousers. "Are you going out there?"

Logan finished with the soiled towel and tossed it aside. "Yeah. I knew Mike Barney fairly well. We were pretty good friends." His eyes went past Doc to the sun-brightened roadway. "I was goin' to take his wife in one of Danforth's buggies but she's goin' out there with someone else." The pale eyes returned solemnly to Doc's face. "Bessie Arnett."

Doc drank a dipperful of water then turned to gaze out into the roadway. Bessie had no business going out there, she'd had all the pain she could stand. He thought of going to see her then decided not to. Despite all his years as a medical man and all the tears and anguish he'd seen because of his profession, he still could not stand to see women cry.

He went to the doorway and looked northward. Neither Padgett nor Hollister were in sight but there was a band of heavily armed rangemen walking their horses southward down Main Street. He recognized Burt Standish and several of the other riders. Mitchell Smith was not among them.

They rode slowly, silent and unsmiling. When they passed the jailhouse every head turned. Doc felt hair on the back of his neck rising.

Will Logan was shrugging into his black coat when he walked up to stand with Doc and watch the horsemen pass. Several of them nodded and were nodded to in return. Then Logan stepped back inside and as Doc was about to head for home, he glanced over his shoulder and saw the sinewy redheaded man buckling a six-gun around his middle. He said, "Leave it, boy. Don't wear that thing today."

Will finished buckling the belt and adjusted his coat to cover it. He did not answer, he simply made a bitter smile at Doc.

The cafe was closed, the roadway door locked, and the old fly-specked shade was pulled down behind the front window.

Walt's new clerk was in the store doorway as Doc passed, and he nodded his head. He had both thumbs hooked in his red suspenders. Doc looked past him, there was no one else in the store so evidently Walt had gone home for the day.

As warm as it was Doc was beginning to feel cold before he reached his gate and turned in. Juniper was like a ghost town. Ordinarily this time of day there was roadway traffic, people on the plankwalks, noise and activity, perhaps even a dogfight or two.

He went to the kitchen for a cup of watered whisky and reproached himself even as he raised the cup to his lips. Tomorrow, he told himself. He would not drink all day tomorrow, and that would be the start of a new leaf.

Sam came by in his ill-fitting black suit, the old Bible weighing heavily in his off-side coat pocket and his old black hat with its ingrained sweat stains brushed free of dust. He rarely smiled on funeral day but at least most of the time when he went up there to read from the Good Book, it was over a box with someone in it who had died in bed. This time and the previous time he'd done his civic duty, the harness maker had been unable to reconcile himself to the idea that what he was doing now was in any way normal.

Doc offered him a cup of watered whisky which Sam accepted gratefully. With the passing of Arley Patton a real hardship had come to visit the town. Sam's lined, leathery countenance looked solemn even after he'd drained the cup, partly because of how he had to spend this afternoon, but also because of something else. "Macklin's crew is in town," he told Doc, "along with the men from Patterson ranch."

Doc nodded.

Sam looked down into his empty cup. "Do you know all it'd take to wipe this town off the

215

map?" Sam waved the empty cup. "One piece of shotgun-wadding or one bullet hittin' a coal oil can, or one feller droppin' a cigarette in the wrong place."

Paul Winthrop had not thought of fire and as he looked at the harness maker now the idea did not register with him as a real threat.

Sam put his cup upon the kitchen table and straightened up. He was a lanky, rawboned older man who at one time had probably been able to go bear hunting with a fly swatter, and he still looked capable. "Why didn't that damned fool get on his horse this morning and just ride away? Two-thirds of the town is dead against him for what he done last night. Now those rangemen are standin' around town down in front of Jim's barn. It's a tinder box, Doc. The whole damned town is a tinder box and having those burials this afternoon is downright incongruous."

Doc's eyes widened slightly. The word had been appropriate but he would have bet a handful of new money that Sam Starr didn't know it. He would have lost the bet. He considered refilling his cup then resolutely put it down and stood remembering something old Jeremiah had told him once about men like Marshal Padgett: *They got straw inside and cold water for blood. Something was left out when they was*

216

made...first-rate killers..." He gazed at Sam Starr wondering why he should care about Jack Padgett, or all the rest of this gawd-awful mess. The answer was directly behind the question: He shouldn't care and maybe he wouldn't care except that any first-rate killer, who also happened to be a very deadly man with weapons, was not going to be shot down without taking others with him. He said, "Sam, did you ever have the feeling that maybe you've lived too long?"

Starr said nothing but he kept his eyes on Doc's face for a long time, then he hitched at his old sagging coat and turned toward the front of the house. Over his shoulder he finally said, "Yeah, lots of times, but I didn't know anyone else ever thought that." Out on the porch he smiled. "We wouldn't bury those outlaws the same day we buried Don and Arley and the others because it wasn't decent to do that. Don an' Arley was upstandin' men in town. But today we're goin' to plant that corralyard hostler right along with those damned outlaws and no one's said a word about that to me.... I guess the thing is that if you own a business instead of just bein' a corralyard hostler you are too upstandin' to be buried with outlaws, eh?"

Doc watched the lanky old man pass beyond his gate on his way out to Cemetery Hill.

217

18

Without having made a conscious decision about attending the burials, Doc brushed his old hat, reshaped it until it was presentable, then put on his black trousers and coat, and snugged up the black tie. Leaving the house he caught sight of Mitchell Smith walking toward his front gate up the west side of Main Street. He closed the door gently and went as far as the gate.

With characteristic frankness Mitchell said, "It's been more than a half hour." Doc gave him a hard look. "Can you see up there on the hill? Four coffins on trestles and a few people."

Mitchell nodded without turning to look.

"Marshall Padgett's up there. So is Sheriff Hollister. And Walt's daughter and the hostler's widow."

Smith turned, grunted, and turned back.

218

"What's Padgett doing up there? He killed that man last night."

Doc made no attempt to answer. "You want to mount up your friends and ride out there and shoot him during a burial ceremony?"

Smith looked stonily at Winthrop. He reminded Doc of a lot of Indians he had known. He was not going to commit himself through words, perhaps because he was both troubled and yet still resolute.

Doc let a long moment pass before speaking again. "You couldn't have set a time limit anyway, Mitchell, even if there wasn't to be any burials today." He wanted to ask Smith to take his rangemen and leave town but he knew better. "I'm going up there. You can come along if you wish."

Smith's response was almost as delayed as Doc's comment had been. "We'll wait," he said, and turned. As Doc was departing Smith turned to look out toward Cemetery Hill again, for a longer interval this time.

Doc shook off a feeling of unreality and started walking, his face tilted toward the hill and the people standing up there. It was a considerable distance but the tall figure of the town marshal and the bearlike figure of the Wyoming lawman were distinguishable. He failed to distinguish between the women because Bessie and Mike

219

Barney's wife were nearly the same size and because both were dressed in black.

He was halfway along when he heard someone coming behind. He paused to look back. The redheaded blacksmith's helper nodded but made no move to increase his gait as Doc resumed walking. They reached the base of Cemetery Hill with about a hundred and fifty feet separating them, and the last time Doc turned he saw Logan's old black coat flop open to disclose the low-worn holstered Colt.

This time there were no musicians. In fact there were two dozen fewer people at the open graves this time. Sam was standing behind the boxes as he usually did, lips moving as he read and reread the passages he would recite. His face was damp, also a little pale beneath its normal ruddy color.

Doc stopped to catch his breath and met the cold, steady gaze of Jack Padgett. Nearby, Ash Hollister was also regarding Doc, but the sheriff's expression was quizzical.

Walt Nevins was up there as were the three men from the corralyard, and although Doc only knew Mike Barney's wife by sight, he thought she looked much older this afternoon.

Bessie did not see the doctor. She was looking out over the town and on westward. Her face was chalk white and her mouth was held in an ugly line. She seemed to be holding herself together with great effort.

Doc let Will Logan pass him on his way toward the others, and saw Marshal Padgett's eyes follow Logan step by step. By now of course Marshal Padgett knew all the other possemen from town had fled.

A third woman came from the far side of the hearse as Sam cleared his throat and cast a troubled look all around before beginning to read. She was the part-Indian wife of the dead caféman.

Doc went woodenly over to join the others as Sam's voice broke the stillness. It was grotesque, he thought; there was such hatred up here he could feel it like white heat.

Walt's eyes were watering, his daughter did not move, did not even seem to be breathing as she continued to stare out over the westward range country. Near her Mike Barney's widow finally lost control and Doc was certain Bessie's fixation on something far off, which no one else could see, was so intense she did not hear the sobs, but she turned and took the widow into her arms and held her like a child.

Sam paused to mop at sweat with a limp handkerchief then resumed his reading. Doc's attention was pulled away by distant movement.

The rangemen were riding up through town.

They paused at the north end where the trail led up to Cemetery Hill. They dismounted and stood at the heads of their horses. Doc's heart sank. He looked askance at Jack Padgett. The marshal had seen them. They were blocking his way back into town and there were eight or nine of them.

Sam stopped reading and without closing the Book also looked down there. Then he closed the Bible, pocketed it and said, "Couple of you gents lend a hand...Bessie you better take Miz' Barney back to town."

Walt stepped beside his daughter and took her arm. The three of them started down the path in the direction of town. Marshal Padgett had not moved but the Wyoming lawman helped lower the coffins while the three men from the corralyard reached for shovels. Not a word was said.

Will Logan was facing the town marshal from a distance of perhaps twenty-five feet and his coat had been brushed back on the right side. Doc's breath caught in his throat. He moved directly in front of Logan, whose mouth flattened with determination.

Marshal Padgett lifted his hat, reset it so that his eyes were protected from the late-day sun, and started down off Cemetery Hill. Sheriff Hollister straightened up from helping with the coffins and seemed about to speak. Sam Starr did not even look around as he said, "Leave it be, Sheriff," and Hollister eyed the lanky older man with the sagging coat pocket.

Will Logan's determined expression altered slightly as he joined the others in watching Marshal Padgett walk without haste in the direction of the distant rangemen. It was a long walk and ahead of him Bessie and the corral-yard hostler's widow were moving more slowly.

Doc finally turned away from the blacksmith's helper and also started forward. Behind him Will Logan spoke quietly. "Don't get too close." Doc ignored it.

The day was near to ending, there were shadows on the far side of stones, trees, even the town below and far ahead. Dusk would arrive in another hour or so. Doc watched the marshal; he had to respect the man. He was walking directly into odds no one could overcome and he was doing it as he had always faced peril, head up, body loose, long legs taking steady strides.

Doc thought of a number of words to describe what he was witnessing but none of them completely captured the drama.

Marshal Padgett was overtaking Bessie and the hostler's widow, who had recovered from the desolation that had overcome her on Cemetery Hill and was now walking beside Bessie unaided, her dark, round face raised slightly, shoulders squared, sturdy, thick body moving steadily but slowly. Doc saw Bessie's face turn. He saw the 'breed woman respond. After that there was no conversation between them. They seemed to be looking down where the rangemen were standing, thumbs hooked, bodies loose, watching people heading away from the graveyard hill.

From a fair distance someone softly called, "Doctor!" It was Ash Hollister and he was taking long strides to catch up. Doc slackened a little but not much. He did not especially want the Wyoming lawman's company right then, but when Hollister reached him and lay a hand on his arm he paused. Hollister jerked his head. "Walk over to one side. Don't be directly behind him." He tugged and Doc yielded to the pressure. They angled to Marshal Padgett's left until Hollister thought they would be out of harm's way, then Hollister looked worriedly down where the women were moving slowly. They were between Marshal Padgett and those rangemen. Doc guessed his worry and said, "They won't do anything as long as Bessie and the other lady are in front of Padgett."

Ash Hollister's facial expression said that he

would never wager his life on that kind of a premise.

The heat was still noticeable even though the sun was very close to disappearing beyond the westerly rims of Piute Valley. Doc was thirsty. He glanced at Hollister, the bearlike lawman had a closed look, a hard slant to his jaw, and his eyes were nearly hidden. He seemed to be watching for some signal or motion or shout that would enable him to anticipate how this was going to end. The rangemen were exactly where they had been for almost an hour now, hip-shot, occasionally making short observations, but most of all measuring distances. They had Winchesters on their saddles but clearly Marshal Padgett was going to walk right on up into handgun range.

He had an advantage that he understood better than anyone else: Everyone who was out there was afraid of him, even some of those rangeriders. He was a dead shot and he was fearless. It would be suicide to allow him to get much closer.

He strode to within thirty feet of Bessie and Mike Barney's widow without bothering to cast a glance in their direction. He had been watching for those rangemen down by the road to fidget, and finally several of them had done it. His mouth flattened into a bitter faint smile and he did not take his eyes off them as he came abreast of Bessie and the hostler's widow. He had never before faced down that many armed men; it was a genuine challenge and when he accomplished it, facing them head-on like this, it would provide food for his soul and his ego for the rest of his life. He would become a legend. The most formidable lawman of them all, greater than the man who had trained him, better than Hickok, Garrett, Dallas Stoudenmire.

His eyes were fixed upon the stocky man who was standing slightly in front of the others. He recognized him as old Jeremiah Macklin's top hand. He was not sure he had ever heard the man's name but it didn't matter. Behind him a couple of cowboys looked left and right, visibly wilting, and not from the heat.

He was getting close to handgun range but not *accurate* handgun range. There was time for a few more of them to wilt as he came on, ivory-stocked six-gun lashed in place, eyes shaded and drawn out narrow. Within a few minutes he would be close enough for what he did best — head shooting.

He knew as did most lawmen that cowboys were not good shots; in their line of work there was seldom time for practicing, and guns were not the tools of their trade anyway.

He had almost forgot the two women until a slight sound on his right side and a couple of feet to the rear distracted him. He turned his face, showing contempt and irritation. The hostler's wife was looking at him from a white face with large dark eyes. Bessie too was staring at him. His mouth curled as he started to face forward and move ahead. The dark woman said his name.

"Marshal Padgett."

He would have ignored her but she was moving toward him so he turned. She was very close and there was no indication at all that she was going to do anything but cry out at him.

The explosion was partially muffled but even so it was loud. Doc stopped in his tracks as did the lawman at his side.

Down by the road the waiting rangemen jerked erect. Farther back Will Logan, walking beside Sam Starr, grunted in surprise.

Bessie was closer than any of them. Her father, who had started toward town with the women, had dropped far back. He could see his daughter's hand fly to her mouth as though to stifle a scream.

The widow stepped back as Doc began moving swiftly toward her. Marshal Padgett staggered in a half turn from the impact and with legs braced raised a hand to the lower side of his white shirt. Doc could see the blood and broke into a trot.

Padgett still had the hand pressed to his side when he raised his head and looked at Mike Barney's widow. She was gripping an under-and-over .41 caliber belly-gun that was nickel plated and had three-inch barrels. Soiled-looking grey powder smoke was still hanging in the breathless air.

Doc arrived slightly winded and lunged to catch Marshal Padgett as his knees began to turn loose. He eased him down and sank to one knee with his body protecting the lawman's face from the dying red sun.

Sheriff Hollister came up, looked and said, "Jesus!"

Jack Padgett did not lose consciousness as Doctor Winthrop went to work with swift, experienced hands. He tore cloth and after exposing the wound and studying it, tore more shirting to create a compress, but nothing would stop the gushing blood.

Padgett's eyes went past Doc to the dark woman. She looked at him, dropped the little gun, and stumbled into Bessie's arms.

Walt Nevins came up as white as a sheet, gathered both women, and began herding them away, down toward the roadway where the stunned horsemen were just now recovering from their astonishment and turning to mount up.

Doc was desperate. He said, "Sheriff, can you carry him? I've got to get him to my house."

Hollister leaned and lifted the wounded man as though he were a child and with Doc hastening ahead they started for the roadway and southward on across it in the direction of the Winthrop place. They ignored everyone including the band of mounted rangemen who rode up and halted. Hollister picked his way through them without once looking up.

About the time they reached Doc's gate the sun finally sank and dusk immediately descended.

19

Doc could not stop the bleeding but he managed to slow it. He watched Marshal Padgett's eyes in anticipation of the dull dryness which would precede death. He got whisky down him and made him as comfortable as he could on his examination-room table and when he looked up, Ash Hollister, standing back out of the way, his shirt-front and trousers drenched with blood, looked back.

The bullet had been fired at very close range, and it had been a large caliber missile. When Doc had placed Padgett on his side to examine the exit hole he was surprised to find that it was very small. Usually a slug like that went in small and came out making a very large hole. This time the procedure had been reversed.

There was black-powder stain on Padgett's shirt and through it on the skin. If Doc had not been out there he still would have described the wound as having been made at very close range, perhaps at a distance of not more than five feet.

He got a folded blanket under the marshal's head for elevation, got more whisky down him, and followed this with laudanum, even though Jack Padgett did not appear to be in great pain. He seemed stunned, even twenty minutes after being shot he seemed completely shocked.

He moved his eyes tiredly from Hollister to Doc. Up until now he had made no attempt to speak. In fact Doc was sure he would die without opening his mouth, but Doc was wrong. Padgett said, "...A woman..."

Doctor Winthrop half-heard that. He was struggling to reach a decision. Padgett was in the same situation Jeremiah Macklin had been in — too weak to be surgically opened in an effort to stop the bleeding and certain to die if the bleeding was not stopped.

As though incapable of believing it Padgett repeated himself. "Shot...by a damned woman."

The incredulity in his voice was noticeable even though the voice itself seemed to be fading. Marshal Padgett closed his eyes.

Hollister looked at his saturated clothing and back to Marshal Padgett's face. That was as long as it was required for Marshal Jack

Padgett to die.

Doc raised the half-empty cup of whisky and downed its contents. He raised his eyes and Sheriff Hollister spoke while gazing at the waxen grey face. "I knew it would end – but not like this. Half the town was out there waiting for him and those stockmen too. I guess he couldn't believe it either."

The whisky had absolutely no effect on Doc as he stood watching the blood. When it no longer flowed, he raised the blanket and covered Marshal Padgett from head to feet, then he sluiced his own hands off in the wash basin and dried them on a little frayed towel. "Thanks for packing him down here, Sheriff."

Hollister blinked as though such a remark surprised him. He eventually said, "Thank gawd I got a change of clothes at the rooming house," and left Doc alone in the examination room.

He went to the kitchen to do a better job of scrubbing, took the little basin with its pinkish water with him and flung its contents out back into the geranium bed. Sitting down at the kitchen table, he felt more exhausted than he could remember feeling in twenty years.

Later, he lighted a couple of lamps, one for the parlor and one for the kitchen.

Mitchell Smith arrived when darkness had

replaced the dusk. With characteristic gravity he looked at Doc and raised only his eyebrows. Doc nodded and led the way to the kitchen. "I'm surprised he was able to hang on as long as he did, Mitchell." Doc stirred himself. "Where is what's-her-name, Mike Barney's widow?"

"I took her and Bessie Arnett to the Nevins's house and sat with them for a while. I guess that's why she acted so torn up before the burials."

"Why?"

"Well, women don't go around with guns in their pockets, do they, Doctor?"

There had been no time to think much about how it had happened. Now that there was, Doc nodded his head. "I guess they don't unless they plan to use a gun ahead of time." He leaned in the chair gazing at the younger man. "How many were out there waiting to kill him — ten, fifteen? But when it happened I couldn't believe the way it happened."

Mitchell Smith looked around the kitchen and Doc interpreted the look correctly. He rose and filled two cups, put one in front of the stockman and took the second one back to the table with him. "You know," he said looking at the cup, "I got to quit this stuff."

Mitchell put his hat atop the table and drank,

then blew out a ragged breath. "Walt's girl is goin' to keep her there at the house for a while. She walked out onto the porch with me and we talked a little." Mitchell paused to solemnly regard the older man. "She don't look strong, does she? Pretty as a speckled bird but not likely to be strong."

Doc drained his cup and pushed it away as he slouched on the table, barely listening. Even his bones felt tired.

"I guess when it came right down to it, though, she had enough guts for both of them. . . . You know what I thought first, Doctor? That Bessie had shot him. Of course we were a fair distance away but I just naturally figured she had the right to shoot the son of a bitch."

Doc raised his head. "Hell, son, half the town had a right to shoot him. . . . Well, Jim Danforth's got one more trip up the hill." He got to his feet and waited for the younger man to do the same. Then he herded Mitchell Smith out to the front porch, blinked at the rash of high stars and breathed deeply for a moment. A sudden thought arrived and he said, "Mitchell, are you goin' to be around town within the next few days? I'd like to talk to you."

Smith was gazing southward down where a few stores were still showing lights. "Yeah. Maybe in a day or two. What did you want

234

to talk about?"

Doc said, "Good night," and left the younger man gazing after him as he went back inside and closed the door. Mitchell shrugged and walked away.

Doc went to bed in his underwear, which he ordinarily did, because over the years he'd had to jump up in response to emergency night calls so often, it seemed ridiculous to him to have to get fully dressed each time. This way he only had to jump into his britches, shirt and coat to be ready to hasten forth.

But not tonight. A lot of lamps glowed until very late throughout town, but no one came banging on Doc's door. He probably would not have heard them anyway.

When he awakened the sun was climbing. He went out back to scrub, shave, and fire up the stove, then he got dressed before returning to start breakfast. He was as hungry as a bitch wolf.

A half hour later as he was cleaning up in the kitchen, Ash Hollister arrived in clean attire and accepted Doc's offer of coffee but lied about having already eaten so that he could tactfully decline Doc's offer of breakfast.

Doc felt fresh for some unfathomable reason so when Hollister mentioned Mike Barney's widow Doc construed his interest as being altruistic and said, "She's goin' to stay with Bessie Arnett for a while. I guess they got something to share and most likely they need each other."

Sheriff Hollister nodded slowly while turning his coffee cup. He finally sighed and said, "Murder is murder, Doctor Winthrop." Doc faced him with widening eyes. Then his color climbed. "What in hell are you talking about, Sheriff?"

Hollister stopped turning the cup and shifted in his chair. "Well, is there another name for what she did — in front of maybe twenty or thirty witnesses?"

Doc sat erectly at the table for a long time before speaking again. "Y'know up until you came along this morning I was feeling pretty good. . . . Mister Hollister, this town's gone through hell lately. Today is the first time in a couple of months there is no need for folks to be scairt. We've lost some of our best citizens and a number of others. We've had nothing but burials around here for a couple of weeks. Now, we got one more to plant and it wasn't murder."

Hollister's deep-set eyes rested upon Paul Winthrop's agitated face. He pushed the untouched cup away and leaned massive arms atop the table. "As far as I know, Doctor, killin' someone for revenge isn't classified as self-defense."

Doc's expression of perplexity deepened. "Sheriff, you sat right here in this house and told me you thought Marshal Padgett was a son of a bitch and probably a murderer, and that was the reason you weren't goin' to hand over the bounty money."

Hollister's reply in his mild voice was terse. "That's right. I don't recollect sayin' he was a son of a bitch but I did say he was most likely a murderer. But that's not what I'm talkin' about. Padgett is over with and done for. He's dead. He was shot at very closer range by a woman whose husband he had killed. He had no idea she was going to shoot him, and under the law because she carried that little pistol up there yesterday to kill him, it's called premeditation. Premeditated murder."

Doc fought to control his rising anger. He drank coffee, put the cup aside, ran bent fingers through his hair, and finally shook his head. "Tell you what I think you'd better do," he said. "Catch the afternoon stage out of Piute Valley and go back where you came from." He forced a deaths-head grin. "Sheriff, if I were in your boots I wouldn't talk like this around town today before you leave."

Hollister leaned upon the table. He was right. He had been a law officer a long time. He knew the law. He raised his eyes to Doc's face. "I'm

not going to try an' arrest her, Doctor. My bailiwick is Wyoming. The only authority I have
down here is the same authority you or anyone
else has — I could make a citizen's arrest. And
I didn't come in here this morning to get you
all upset. I just wanted to make a point of law."

Doc rose as he said, "You've made it, Sheriff,"
and took his guest through the house and left
him standing alone on the front porch.

He was so mad he did not hear someone
knocking on the door until the noise grew
louder, and when he went out there he was in
a bad mood. The caller was Swen Jorgenson
who took one look at Doc's face and started to
back away. "I can come back later, Doctor, I
only wanted to measure Mister Padgett."

Doc caught the carpenter's arm and pulled
him inside. He pointed to a closed door and
said, "He's in there," then Doc went out onto
his porch and did some deep breathing. By the
time Swen joined him Doc's blood pressure
had gone down a lot.

As Swen was leaving Doc gazed southward.
There was no roadway traffic but the plankwalks had people on them, which had not been
the case lately. Someone kicked open the saloon
doors and swept out a great cloud of dust. He
was a thick man with a flour-sack apron around
his ample middle, and Doc recognized him

even from that distance. Jim Danforth.

Doc was turning to enter the house when a familiar ringing sound came from farther south over on the opposite side of Main Street where Will Logan was shaping steel over the anvil.

Doc avoided the cups on his kitchen table and got his hat. As he left the house he also took along his satchel. Walter Nevins was across the road. They waved and Doctor Winthrop waited for the late-morning stage to pass northward before stepping off the plankwalk. There was one passenger. He and she exchanged a look before the coach passed by. It was the cafeman's widow. He stood a moment gazing after the coach, saddened by the look on the widow's face, saddened too by her obvious decision to leave Piute Valley.

The morning was clear and turning warm. There seemed to be some clouds forming beyond the distant rims off toward the northeast but if there was rain in them it would probably not reach Juniper for several days.

As Doc turned the corner up where the public corrals were someone called to him from the roadway. It was the Patterson Ranch rangeboss, Burt Standish. He was coming into town from the north on a wide-eyed dapple colt in a hackamore. The big colt seemed ready to turn inside out at the first loud noise. Doc returned to the edge of the plankwalk as Burt reined over and halted. Doc eyed the horse askance but Standish lounged in the saddle as though he were atop an old broke animal. He considered Doc for a moment then said, "That was the damnedest thing I ever saw." Doc nodded; he had no doubt about the meaning of that cryptic remark. "And I got to thinking last night... Juniper needs another lawman."

Doc nodded again, beginning to suspect where this conversation was going.

Burt leaned on the saddlehorn looking serious. "Before I went to work on the ranch I was a deputy sheriff in Idaho for six years. That's why I rode into town today."

Doc squinted upward. "Burt, are you talkin' about filling out Marshal Padgett's term?"

"Yes."

"Well, I can give you the names of the men on the town council and you can go around and talk to them, but I'm just one member of the council. I can't tell you yes or no."

Standish was satisfied with that and listened as Doc named the members he should see, then he smiled. "I'm obliged," he said, and reined away. The big dapple colt took three steps and bogged his head, squealed, and took to Burt Standish with a will. Doc watched as the colt bucked completely across to the opposite plankwalk and scattered several people over there before turning back toward Doc. Burt lost his hat but sat the saddle as though he did this every day. When the colt suddenly rammed down to a stiff-legged halt less than fifteen feet from Doc, who was preparing to flee, Burt looked around for his hat then faced Doc. "Would it be all right," he asked, "if I mentioned your name to the other council members?"

Doc stared. "What about this damned horse?" he growled. "Aren't you going to overhaul his plumbing for trying to hurt you?"

Burt smiled. "He's just a colt, Doc. If he'd been a spoiled horse I'd overhaul him, but he just don't know any better. He'll settle down in a month or so."

Doc eyed the horse then wagged his head. "Sure, mention my name," he replied, and walked away thinking that a man who wouldn't larrup hell out of a green colt would probably make a good town marshal, because he would be equally as unlikely to use a gun when it was not necessary.

20

In contrast to the other burials, the one at dusk atop Cemetery Hill required everyone who was up there — Doctor Winthrop, Jim Danforth and Sam Starr — to lower the box after Starr had read his Bible. Then they put aside coats and pitched in shoveling the dirt. It was hard work, none of them were as young as they had once been, and none of them had done that kind of manual labor in years so they rested a lot, leaning on shovels gazing pensively down toward the lighted town. The last time they halted to mop off sweat and catch their breath, Starr spoke without taking his eyes off the distant town and also as though he were not addressing either of his companions, just himself.

"Four horsethieves, Cal Vincent, three store-robbers, Mike Barney from the corralyard. . . . That makes ten men he killed, don't it?"

Danforth growled. "No, it makes nine, and you're forgetting those two he brought in last year with the beat-up man. He killed eleven men."

Doc went back to work with his shovel. "You want to spend the night up here? Let's get this job finished."

They worked for a while, finally mounding the grave and moving around tamping it into the prescribed rounded shape, high enough to allow for natural settling. Doc stopped to look around. There was a double row of fresh graves, all properly mounded. "I never saw anything like this," he said, considering each mound individually before moving to the next one. The light was not good but it was adequate for someone standing among all those fresh mounds of tamped earth. "If there'd been an epidemic Juniper probably would not have had so many fresh graves."

Jim Danforth, using a huge blue bandana to wipe off sweat, twisted slightly from the middle to gaze at the other graves. Then he stowed the bandana with a loud sigh. "What upset me so bad...over there, that skinny drifter who worked for me. Plumb innocent. Never did anything to deserve bein' shot in the back. And next to him the cafeman." He paused to look at his companions. "And old Jeremiah Macklin...

didn't have a chance. An' those are the ones outlaws shot down, that don't count the ones Marshal Padgett killed. It's goin' to take me a while to get used to what happened in town."

Doc remembered a term he'd heard and repeated it. "A slaughter ground." Then he leaned on his shovel handle eyeing the other two. "Burt Standish talk to you gents today?"

He had, both Sam and Jim nodded but said nothing, and because Doc thought their silence might have something to do with their individual reservations, he said, "I think he'll make a good town marshal."

Danforth looked at the ground. "Well, Doctor, he said he'd had a little experience over in Idaho, but that was a long time ago an' since then he's been a rangeboss." Jim raised his eyes to Doc's face. "You wouldn't hire a blacksmith to repair your pocket watch would you? We need a professional lawman."

Doc's eyes glowed sardonically in the starlight. "Yeah," he said sourly. "Look around you, Jim. We had a professional lawman. If we get another one he might finish up wipin' out the town. Besides, Burt knows everyone. Folks like him, as far as I know, and by gawd if you want to propose hiring another professional lawman at the council meeting I'll tell you flat out I'll vote against it, and I'll propose Burt."

Sam, who had been leaning on his shovel handle solemnly eyeing his friends, turned, expectorated, then turned back and stooped to retrieve his coat and hat. He shrugged into the coat, dumped the hat carelessly atop his mane of iron grey hair, and slung the shovel over his shoulder as he gazed down toward the rooftops and lights of town. "Give Burt a chance," he said to Jim Danforth without looking at him. Then he looked around. "I can sure think of better places to talk than up here." He started down off the hill, adding another sentence. "I got a bottle of malt whisky at the shop if you fellers would care to join me." He neither looked back to see if they were following nor said another word.

It was a long walk back, all three of them had been using muscles they had not used in years, but the real stiffness would not bother them until in the morning. Danforth watched the harness maker for a moment then called to him. "Sam! Ride back with Doc an' me. There's plenty of room on the hearse."

Starr stopped and turned, eyed the hearse and dryly said, "The day'll come when I can't keep you from puttin' me into that thing, but until then...I'll walk." He turned on down off Cemetery Hill.

Doc and Jim climbed to the seat of the hearse,

and as Jim eased off the binders and talked to the horses, Doc lost sight of Sam Starr whose long legs were moving freely, even though tomorrow he most likely would be unable to step over a piece of kindling wood.

Danforth got settled comfortably with the lines in his hands. Doc was dwarfed by Jim's size as he sat hunched, watching big black horse-rumps. The road going down was easier than it had been going up, but even so it still had ruts and they were less visible in the pale-lighted night. Jim hit a few deep ones and as he recovered each time he swore. They were nearing the lower flat country when Doc said, "Burt will do a good job."

Danforth was quiet until they were angling over toward the rear of town. "All right, I'll vote for him if you make the motion to hire him, but I got to tell you flat out, Doctor, I got reservations."

Doctor Winthrop glanced up the roadway as they crossed from the east side of town toward the livery barn. There was not a soul abroad, at least he did not see anyone. As they hauled down out front of the barn Doc said, "Hurry up. I need a drink of that malt whisky."

Danforth climbed ponderously down. "Lend me a hand," he said. "My new hired man don't work nights."

Finally, as Doc bent under the burden of a massive set of harness, his back sent pain from his hips to the back of his head. He staggered to the harness room, shoved the harness on a rack, and was leaning there when Jim came in with the second set. Jim grunted from beneath his burden and looked at Doc. "Back, eh?" he said, and rummaged in a battered old box on the floor with leather hinges. He straightened up triumphantly offering Winthrop a brown bottle. "Rub some of this on it and by morning you'll be good as new."

Doc eyed the bottle. "I don't need a damned liveryman to tell me what to do for a sore back." He took the bottle, removed the cap, sniffed, and jerked his head back. "That's nothing but a blister."

Danforth agreed. "Yep. After you rub it on don't cover it or it will blister you for a fact."

Doc handed back the bottle and went to the door, his back beginning to feel better. They went northward on the same side of the road as the jailhouse and when they were abreast of it they both turned their heads but neither man said a word. The jailhouse door was locked from the outside, it was dark and utterly silent on the inside.

Sam Starr had shed his black attire and was awaiting their arrival behind his counter where he had a bottle and three tin cups. There was an overhead lamp which was smoking because Sam rarely trimmed wicks when he should. They ignored the lamp as Sam splashed brown whisky into the cup and pushed the bottle away. He leaned on his counter eyeing them. Doc was looking at the tin cup. A man couldn't slack off on this stuff if everytime someone offered him a drink he took it.

They downed the first one in silence but as Sam was refilling the cups he said, "This one's to Arley and Don."

They downed that one too. Sam poured again. "To the corralyard feller; what was his...Mike Barney. I remember it now, Mike Barney."

Jim gazed into his cup without touching it. At this rate by the time they got through giving everyone a send-off who'd been killed and buried lately, he and Doc would have to crawl home on all fours. Sam lived in a lean-to room off his shop so he wouldn't have much trouble. Danforth picked up his cup. "Here's to them all, every damned one of them once and for all."

Sam's weathered face screwed up into a scowl. "No. Not them horsethieves nor those boys who raided the town and killed Arley and the rest. Not in the same breath as the decent ones, Jim. And I'm not goin' to drink to Marshal Padgett."

248

Danforth held his raised cup for a moment, then slowly lowered it. "Sam, we've already drunk to the decent ones; Arley and Don and all."

"No we ain't, Jim. How about Mister Macklin?...Isn't that right, Doc? And that cowboy who worked for Patterson ranch — Cal Vincent."

Doc was leaning on the counter looking straight ahead; he didn't enter the dispute. How in the hell did you tell a man he was the illegitimate son of the man he had worked for?

"Doc? *Doc!*"

Winthrop gave a little start. "What? What are you yelling about, Sam?"

"I'm not yelling, you're just gettin' deaf. I said we hadn't ought to drink to Marshal Padgett and Mister Macklin in the same breath as them outlaws and horsethieves."

Doctor Winthrop focused his attention upon this issue while clutching his cup. Then, instead of answering the harness maker he said, "Do you know what this stuff does to your insides? I've seen dissected corpses of people who've drunk themselves to death. Even the brain....One time I saw a skull that had been opened and—"

Danforth, who now owned a saloon, turned on the smaller and older man with a savage scowl and Sam Starr leaned far over his counter, teeth bared. "Are you sayin' my malt whisky isn't good quality, Doctor Winthrop?" he snarled and before Doc could reply Danforth leaned his fleshy face close to Doc. "You got any idea what that kind of talk could do to my new business, you darned old billy goat?"

Doc considered the pair of hostile faces and raised his tin cup. "Here's to a couple of good friends: Sam and Jim."

Starr was not altogether appeased. "What about Mister Macklin and that Patterson cowboy, whatever in hell his name was?"

Doc did not even blink. "Them too.... All the decent, honest, upstandin', respectable... Sam, that lamp is going out."

Starr had to lean far over his counter to look downward, but Jim Danforth only had to turn sideways to see the floor where Doc was lying. Starr clucked. "Spilt the whisky all over.... What's wrong with him, Jim?"

Danforth leaned, but had to brace himself with one big hand, gripping the edge of the harness shop counter. "He went and passed out, Sam. A feller told me one time doctors can't handle it. Doctors, Irishmen an' In'ians. Come around from back there and give me a hand. We got to take him up to his house."

Starr was still leaning far over looking solemnly downward. "Why?" he asked. "What we got to do that for?"

Jim straightened up irritably, now gripping the counter with both hands. "Because, confound it, if we don't he'll pee all over himself and your floor. That's why. Now come around and lend me a hand."

Sam pushed backward until he was erect, then he too reached for the counter. He put a glazed look over Danforth's head to the dingy far wall, wearing the expression of a man listening to voices no one else could hear. He sadly said, "Can't do it."

Danforth glared. "What do you mean you can't do it? You know just half of what this scrawny old goat has done for this town? You got any idea how much folks owe him for all he's done?"

Sam's eyes did not come off the far wall to Danforth's red, sweaty face. "I mean if I let go of this counter I'm goin' down too."

Danforth watched the harness maker for a moment then forgot about Doc on the floor and looked into his tin cup. "Sam, if that's malt whisky I'll eat my hat. Where did you get it?"

"Last spring when those traders came through with that mule train," replied Starr, trying without much success to enunciate clearly.

Danforth's eyes widened. "...Of all the

damned. . . You bought whisky off In'ian traders? Look at yourself! How old are you? By gawd you're old enough to know what traders put into that whisky they trade to the In'ians. . . . Sam, where are you?"

Danforth had to stand on his toes to lean far enough over the counter to look downward where Sam had gone the moment he loosened his hold on the counter.

Danforth dropped back down and considered Doctor Winthrop. "And harness makers," he said. "Doctors, Irishmen, In'ians and harness makers. Come on, Doc, sit up so's I can get a grip on you and I'll carry you home."

Doc did not sit up so Jim knelt and, using both big hands, got Paul Winthrop leaning against the counter like a grain sack. He flexed his big arms, held his breath, and with a loud grunt got Doc over his shoulder. Then he stood up and steadied himself on the counter before turning in the direction of the door.

Night air usually helped and it did as Jim Danforth cleared the harness works door and turned northward with his inert burden. Winthrop was a slight man and Jim Danforth was a large, thick man, running to fat now but still with the vestiges of the powerful build and strength he'd once had. What he was never able to figure out afterward was why the other two had turned loose all over and he hadn't. Nor was he ever afterward able to recollect a single thing after he walked out of Sam Starr's shop.

He dumped Doc on his own examination table and departed, breathing hard from exertion. The night was beginning to hold a little chill, so it was late, past the middle of the night, in fact, before Danforth closed the door and walked down from Doc's porch. He hitched up his shoulders, aimed across the road in the direction of the saloon, and proceeded with the elaborate dignity of someone who was drunk and did not want others to notice this, putting one foot in front of the other with considerable care.

There was no one to notice. The town had retired long ago. The only witness to Danforth's progress was a bony-tailed, slab-sided brindle dog who had been rummaging in garbage bins out back and had been drawn to the roadway by the sound of someone walking.

21

When Doc awakened it was almost noon and he ached in places he did not even know he had, but his head and stomach were the worst. He did not move a finger for a long while, just lay back squinting at the ceiling. When it finally occurred to him that he was on his own hard table in the examination room with nothing under him, he groaned and sat up, placed both feet firmly upon the floor and pushed.

He made it to the kitchen and put the coffee pot on a stove burner, coaxed a little fire to burn, and sat down at the table, exhausted.

An hour later, with hot black coffee in him, he returned to the examination room for some powders which he mixed in water and drank. The powders helped but not for fifteen minutes.

He remembered everything up to the point when he and Jim Danforth had gone up to the harness works. He knew what his trouble was and shuddered at the thought of ever taking another drink. He went to the bedroom and dropped face-down upon the quilts and slept until late afternoon, then he arose to go out back to the bath house and soak in hot water for an hour.

Gradually, as his stomach and head worked their way back to normalcy, he began to recall more of what had happened last night and by the time he returned indoors to climb into clean attire and consider his face in a wall mirror he recalled that bottle of malt whisky. The haggard face looking back from the mirror made him look away. He drank another glassful of water with medicinal powders, and by suppertime — although he was not the least bit hungry — he was feeling fairly well, except for a sore back, aching joints, stiff shoulders and swollen hands, the result of all that shovel work last night.

He made a fresh pot of coffee and was stoking the fire box of the kitchen stove when someone rattled his roadway door. He went out there expecting either Starr or Danforth. It was Mitchell Smith. Doc gazed at him from the clean hat down to the axle-greased boots. Smith was wearing a new blue work shirt and clean trousers.

255

In the last couple of months many things had changed; too many things probably, but in the process some promising new things were taking root. He knew for a fact that Mitchell Smith and Bessie Arnett had seen each other dozens of times over the years but until yesterday, while several men were being buried and another man was walking down to get himself killed, they had evidently never considered anything closer, and in fact Doc had been on his porch with that Wyoming lawman and had seen Bessie jerk away from Smith yesterday in the early afternoon. Last evening, however, they had met to help a third person struggle with anguish. Doc did not believe that Mitch had come to town just to see him.

Doc opened the door wider for Smith to enter. Beyond, out in the roadway, a saddlehorse was tethered to the hitch rail. The sun was going down but it would be awhile yet before daylight departed.

Smith faced Doc in the parlor and with his customary directness said, "You said you wanted to talk to me."

Doc nodded. "Care for some coffee? I'm brewing a fresh pot."

The went out to the kitchen, and Doc motioned for his guest to seat himself at the table, then he found two clean cups and filled them with coffee. As he took them to the table he said, "We buried Marshal Padgett last night."

Mitch Smith accepted that without comment and studied Doc's face. Finally he said, "You need a vacation, Doctor."

Doc nodded absently. That wasn't at all what he needed, what he had to do was turn over a new leaf and get rid of some bad habits. While gazing at his coffee he said, "Have you gone through Jeremiah's papers?"

Smith's brows pulled slightly inward. "No. That's for a judge or a lawyer to do."

Doc continued to regard the coffee. Damn Jeremiah anyway; Doc's job was patching people – not doing the kind of thing Jeremiah had dropped in his lap. "Well, you most likely had better send for a lawyer, Mitchell."

Smith nodded curtly. "Yes."

"Jeremiah may have left a will, that's why I asked if you'd gone through his papers. In all the years I knew him he never once mentioned kinfolk, but there may have been some." Doc finally lifted his head. "Do you know of any?"

Mitchell took a long time answering. "All I can tell you is that he was married for a long time, his wife died, and they didn't have any children. But if either one of them had kinfolk back east or somewhere else he never mentioned it to me."

"I don't think he had any," stated Doc, watching the younger man. He drummed the table-top and cleared his throat, then rose to get the pot and bring both their cups to the brim again. When he sat down Mitchell was eyeing him with a peculiar expression. He said, "Doctor, if you're worrying about what's to become of the ranch. .so am I. I guess I'd better send for that lawyer maybe tomorrow or the next day. Someone with the authority's got to go through things and set a sales price."

Doc went back to considering his coffee. "You were with him a long while."

"Since I was sixteen. I'm thirty-two now."

Doc nodded slightly. "Sixteen years. In all that time he must have said something to you about the ranch."

"He did; we talked about the ranch every few days. Sometimes when we rode out together, sometimes at the bar here in town. When prices dropped he—"

"I mean, he must have mentioned something about what was to happen to the ranch after he died."

Mitchell Smith's bronzed features showed a sad little smile. "He wasn't ever goin' to die."

"So he never said anything? He never mentioned relatives?"

"No."

Doc lifted the cup and tasted the coffee. It was not as bad as his coffee usually was, perhaps because this time when he brewed it he had not simply tossed another fistful of new coffee over the grounds of the old coffee. He glanced at the younger man over the rim of the cup. Mitchell Smith shifted on the chair, he was becoming impatient. Doc put the cup aside and pulled down a deep breath. He was girding himself for what he had to tell the younger man when Mitch Smith abruptly said, "Bessie Arnett's makin' up a hamper, we're going for a buggy ride this evening. I — uh — that's really why I came into town this afternoon, Doctor. I expected to see you too because you mentioned a meeting, but I guess I'd better get on down and rent a rig from Mister Danforth." He leaned to rise and for a wild moment Doc thought of letting him go, but that passed and he said, "This won't take long." Having made that announcement Doc drank the rest of his coffee. He was feeling almost normal again, as long as he did not move.

"I'm pretty sure Jeremiah didn't have any outside kinfolk, Mitchell. If you don't want to go through his papers I'll drive out and do it. Maybe that ought to be done before you send for a lawyer, because if he left a will you might not need one."

259

Mitch Smith was looking closely at Doctor Winthrop.

Doc spread his hands. "Someone has to go through his papers."

"The lawyer."

Doc took a final deep breath. "Maybe not. . . . He did have an heir."

Smith's intent look remained. "You're sure?"

"Yes," Doc said, and cleared his throat again. "Tell me about your folks, Mitchell."

Now, Smith's expression underwent a slow change as he sat regarding the older man. He did not speak for a while, then he said, "My mother died when I was fifteen. That was down in Taos, New Mexico. Her name was Elizabeth Mitchell. That's where I got my first name." Smith stopped and stared hard at Doctor Winthrop. "Have you heard this before?"

Doc shook his head. He'd had no idea who Mitchell's mother had been. That had not been included in the cryptic statement Jeremiah had made to him the day old Jeremiah was shot.

The younger man continued speaking, his voice flat and terse. "She gave me the name Smith."

"That was her husband's name?"

"No. She was never married."

Doc looked into his cup. It was empty. He thought of going to the stove for a refill, but

Mitchell spoke again in that flat, terse tone of voice.

"Jeremiah Macklin was my father."

Doc almost stopped breathing for a moment, his round eyes fixed upon the younger man's face. "You knew that?"

"Yes, I knew it. Before she died my mother told me about the cowman who came down to Taos from Piute Valley to take delivery on some purebred bulls."

"She told you he was up here?"

"Yes. When she knew she was dying she told me to come up here and tell him who I was . . . I came up here like she said, and got hired on, but I never told Jeremiah the rest of it."

"Aw hell," Doc sighed. "Well, the day your father died he told me he was your father. But I'm sure he had no idea that you knew that. That's what I wanted to talk to you about today." Doc sighed again. This made it a lot easier, but it had been a surprise to him as well. He leaned back and as they sat gazing at one another Doc said, "I'm sorry, Mitchell."

Smith gently shook his head. "Nothing to be sorry about. I guess couldn't either one of us bring ourselves to tell the other one, but all the time I was growing up he treated me like a son, and I was glad to settle for that because I didn't want to embarrass him — or myself."

261

"... Sixteen years. He had to be fond of you, Mitchell."

"Maybe. I was right fond of him."

"You didn't hold anything against him?"

"No. Doctor, the only person I ever really sat in judgment on in my life was Marshal Padgett."

Doc looked out a window, dusk was close. He turned with a smile. "Don't keep Bessie waiting," he said, arising stiffly. "I'll go out front with you." When they were on the porch Doc slapped Mitchell lightly on the shoulder. "Be kind to her, son. She's had more heartache in her young life than a lot of folks have that're three times as old."

Mitchell looked steadily at the older man. "I'll never treat her and Jamie any other way. . . . Doctor? Who else knows?"

"Not a living soul but me — and you. If you want to confide in someone some time that'll be up to you. I never will."

Doc watched the young man go down to the hitch-rack and called quietly after him. "I'll be out tomorrow."

Smith nodded, mounted, turned, and headed in the direction of Jim Danforth's barn. There was still an hour or so of warm daylight left. Doc sat down on a porch chair and relaxed his carcass one limb at a time. Maybe it hadn't

262

been necessary for them to confide in each other. As Mitchell had said, it would have caused an enduring embarrassment between them. For a man no older than he was, Mitchell Smith had a good head on his shoulders.

He was still sitting out there in the warm late evening when the buggy went past at a trot. It was the same one with the yellow running gear he had seen Bessie go by in another time, with a different man, but that other time it had been moving more slowly. This time the passengers didn't see him up there in the dark on the porch.

He went indoors, lighted two lamps, and headed for the kitchen because now, finally, he was hungry. Just before leaving the parlor he winked at the fading portrait on the mantel of a handsome woman, and as always she smiled back.

A hot meal made all the difference, but even the following morning when he arose, the stiffness was still there. He did not take his satchel as he left the house and hiked down to the livery barn where Danforth's new hired man greeted him with a broad, freckled smile. Doc's buggy was neither new nor elegant, and it had never had yellow running gear — it had the same dull red gear it had come with. And the big old horse that pulled his buggy was past the age of surprises and never shied.

It was a magnificent morning. Doc enjoyed every mile of it. By the time he reached the Macklin place he had only one genuine worry in the world, but as Mitch Smith came over to greet him at the rail in front of the barn, Doc did not allow any of that anxiety to show.

They went to the main house. Mitch showed him to Jeremiah's bedroom and the adjoining office, and then he leaned in the doorway as though his entry would be some form of violation. Doc saw him watching and sat down at Jeremiah's dusty old disorderly desk as he said, "Come help if you want to, or pull up a chair and sit here while I do this."

Smith considered a framed picture of Jeremiah's wife on a small table and said, "Somethin' I've always wondered about. . . . Why didn't they get married?"

Doc had no problem guessing who he meant even though Mitch was looking at the picture of the woman who had not been his mother. "We'll most likely never know, Mitchell, but if neither one of them wanted to say, I guess it was a good reason."

The light brown eyes came back to Doc. "Bessie thinks the world of you, did you know that?"

Doc eyed an untidy pile of papers. Statements

like that were always embarrassing. "An' I think the world of her. Mitchell, if I'm holding you up from your work..."

The rangeboss nodded, smiled slightly, and departed.

Doc went to work. Halfway through he was struck by the fact that old Jeremiah had evidently never thrown a piece of paper away if it had writing on it. And it was equally as evident that once having stuffed papers into a desk drawer, he rarely — if ever — looked at them again; the proof of this lay in the fact that there was a fully lined mouse nest made of shredded paper in a lower desk drawer. The family had long since departed and since then nothing had disturbed the nest.

Doc had a sinking sensation when he lifted out the chewed papers and found one that had been painstakingly written in Jeremiah's ponderously large print.

It was a will.

One side and several inches of the top of the paper had been chewed to pieces. Doc lifted out the entire mess, swept the nest into a basket, and sat down again to see if the mother mouse had eaten anything critical.

She had come perilously close at the bottom of the page where tiny rodent teeth marks had skirted just below Jeremiah's signature. Doc pressed the paper flat and read it, then re-read it.

"To my natural son whose mother was Elizabeth Mitchell. . ." It was all there in that heavy, rounded handwriting; everything including all livestock, equipment, land and buildings was bequeathed to Mitchell Smith, old Jeremiah's "natural son".

Doc fished for his handkerchief, blew lustily, put up the handkerchief, and leaned back in the chair to relax. In a quiet voice he addressed the far wall. "You did exactly right, you confounded old horned toad. I'm proud of you just like I was always proud we were friends."

He continued to sit there for a long time and only roused himself when he heard someone coming through the house wearing spurs.

When Mitchell appeared in the doorway Doc beckoned him to the desk and handed him the piece of paper. Then he rose, slapped Mitchell on the shoulder, and went as far as the door before speaking.

"No need to send for a lawyer. I'll see you in town one of these days."

He had to harness the mare by himself but at least this time his California harness was much lighter than the last set he'd struggled with.

The drive back was a little warmer than the drive out had been, but it was still a beautiful day. Heat-haze obscured the distant rim-rock boundaries of Piute Valley and by the time he had Juniper's rooftops in sight he was thirsty, but even that plus the sore shoulders, back and legs could not distract from the sense of pleasure he felt as he pulled off so as to reach town from the lower end, down in back of the livery barn.

After leaving his outfit with the freckled-face young man, who was now running Jim Danforth's barn, Doc went up to the general store and got a dipperful of water under the calm gaze of Walt Nevins and his clerk with the red suspenders. Walt said, "Deliver another baby, did you?"

Doc pointed to a box of cigars and put a five cent piece on the counter. "No. Just wanted to smell grass and look at blue sky."

Walt looked owlishly on as Doc lighted the cigar and held it forth to watch smoke rise. Walt had never seen Doctor Winthrop smoke before in all the years they had known each other. Catching the storekeeper's look Doc said, "A man once told me the best way to give up a vice is to acquire a different one."

Nevins nodded without the faintest notion of what Doc was talking about. Finally, to get the conversation back to something he knew about, Walt said, "Sam Starr's down in bed today. He locked up the shop and taken to his bed."

Doc considered the cigar. "Serves him right," he said and walked away leaving Walt in another quandary.

During the late afternoon Burt Standish arrived out front with a rangeman on some straw in the ranch wagon. Doc went out to look at the man. He had a badly sprained back but between them they got him into the examination room. As Doc peeled off the man's upper garments he asked how the rider had been injured.

"Damned horse threw me," the cowboy said. His color was good but each time he moved he seemed to catch his breath. "Same horse that busted the leg of that young feller a couple of months back."

Doc shifted his gaze from the injured man to Burt, and the Patterson-ranch rangeboss made a little deprecating gesture. Doc was not satisfied with that. "You goin' to keep that horse until he's crippled up half the riders in the country?" Burt reddened. "You're goin' to be running a convalescent home out there, Burt, if you don't get rid of him."

Standish avoided Doc's face. "Other men have rode him since that kid busted his leg."

Doc snorted. "All that proves is that the horse don't always break in two. I'm no horseman but I've been around them all my life and I've seen a lot of spoiled horses, Burt. The smartest ones do that — wait until they can really wreck someone, then take to them like a demon."

"All right," Standish said, looking at his injured man. "I'll have someone take him up a canyon and shoot him."

Doc made a careful examination because he particularly wanted to determine that there was no damage to the spinal column. Each time he probed, the cowboy's jaw muscles would tighten, and that was what Doc watched for. Trying to get one of these rough-and-ready rangemen to admit to pain was worse than pulling teeth.

He stepped back and said, "I'll tell you something about backs, gents. Once you injure one it don't ever let you forget it."

The cowboy rolled his head toward Doc. "Is something broke?"

Doc shook his head. "No. The bones are in place, but you've got some badly bruised muscles. You won't be able to sit a horse for a month, maybe more, and if you get bucked off again you're goin' to have back trouble the rest of your life." Doc caught Standish's attention. "No horsebacking for him, no digging, no lifting."

Burt nodded but the cowboy scowled at Doc. "How do I make a living, for Chris'sake? All I ever did was ride and tend bar."

Doc considered the man. Well-muscled with a thatch of curly dark hair, he was not young, but neither was he old. "Mister," he said, "you're getting long in the tooth for cowboying. Yes, I know, you're as good now as you were at twenty. They all are." Doc stepped closer to the table and faced the cowboy with a hard look. "I don't expect you to take my advice. Why should you do it, no one else does. Quit, draw your money and quit riding. At best, with that back, you won't ever be able to do it again as you've done in the past. . . . Do you know Jim Danforth?"

The cowboy shook his head so Burt Standish explained that Danforth owned the livery barn, then the cowboy's face brightened. "Yeah. Well, I don't exactly know him but I know who he is. He owns the barn here in town."

"Yes, and he also owns the saloon now. Go tell him about your experience as a barman."

The cowboy gazed steadily at Doc. "Is he lookin' for a barman?"

Doc shrugged. "The best way to get an answer to that is to go over and ask him. Now then, don't swivel around when you sit up and put your feet to the floor. Burt, give him a hand." Doc stood back to watch. When the rider was able to stand he made a little grimace, then walked cautiously as far as the door.

270

He was in pain. Doc could have dosed him with laudanum, instead he cautioned him about twisting suddenly, or making any quick moves at all. As the cowboy went very carefully out to the porch Doc tapped Burt's arm. "One dollar."

Burt squinted. "He was on that table only fifteen minutes."

"Yeah, I know, and for him it's free. You're the idiot that let this happen, not him. One dollar."

Standish got red in the face but he dug out a silver cartwheel and handed it over. As Doc pocketed it he said, "Don't let that man anywhere near a riding horse. Don't let him use a shovel or lift anything, or even twist sideways or you're goin' to have him on the ranch as a boarder for a long while. . . . Take him over to see Jim Danforth."

Doc went out as far as the porch to watch them very slowly cross the road and move southward on the far plankwalk.

Later, with a soft summer evening on the way, he was on the front porch when that same top-buggy with the yellow running gear tooled past at a smart little trot and two people saw Doc this time and leaned to grin and wave. He waved back and was watching the rig when Jim Danforth came through the gate. He, too, was looking northward and when he reached the porch steps he said, "Wasn't that Jeremiah's rangeboss and Walt's girl?"

Doc nodded and pointed to a chair. "They make a right smart pair wouldn't you say?"

Danforth eased his bulk down gently. "I guess so. I didn't know they was sparking."

Doc sighed and glanced at the big man. "How is Sam?"

Danforth's expression was rueful. "Fair enough, I guess. He don't look very good but I guess folks don't die from a few drinks of panther piss, do they? You know what that stuff was, Doc?"

"Sam said it was malt whisky."

Danforth snorted. "That was trade liquor, the worst stuff on earth. Sam got it off'n some traders last spring." Jim looked around. "How do you feel?"

Doc felt fine. In fact it had been many months since he had even come close to feeling as good as he felt now. He also did not believe Danforth had come to sit on his porch because he had no place else to go. "Do you have a barman?" he asked.

Jim's face brightened. "I want to thank you for sendin' me that feller. It's been worryin' me ever since I got the saloon, my not havin' experience at all. He's pleasant. I think he'll do just fine and I sure needed someone like him. I come up here to tell you any time you want a drink at my bar, Doc, it's on the house. I'm beholden to you."

Doc thought a moment then said, "How about if I let you keep the whisky and you let me have a free cigar now and then?"

Jim was rising and turned to look quizzically at Doctor Winthrop. "Sure. Free cigar any time you come by, if that's how you want it."

Doc watched the large man go down to the gate, beyond it, and cross the roadway on a diagonal course.